**"You can't force me to go with you,"
she said, throwing one last desperate
statement into the air between them.**

"I will carry you on board myself, Francesca, if you insist on acting like a child."

"I'll scream until someone notices—"

"And sentence your Jacques to certain death? I think not."

"I hate you," she whispered, turning to watch the city slide by before he could see a tear fall.

His voice, when he finally spoke, was as soft as satin, as hard as the *Corazón del Diablo*. "Then perhaps we understand one another after all."

Francesca closed her eyes. She understood, all right. Understood that she'd just sold her soul to the devil.

All about the author...
Lynn Raye Harris

LYNN RAYE HARRIS read her first Harlequin romance novel when her grandmother carted home a box from a yard sale. She didn't know she wanted to be a writer then, but she definitely knew she wanted to marry a sheikh or a prince and live the glamorous life she read about in the pages. Instead, she married a military man and moved around the world. She's been inside the Kremlin, hiked up a Korean mountain, floated on a gondola in Venice and stood inside volcanoes at opposite ends of the world.

These days Lynn lives in North Alabama with her handsome husband and two crazy cats. When she's not writing, she loves to read, shop for antiques, cook gourmet meals and try new wines. She is also an avowed shoeaholic and thinks there's nothing better than a new pair of high heels.

Lynn was a finalist in the 2008 Romance Writers of America Golden Heart contest, and she is the winner of the Harlequin® Presents Instant Seduction contest. She loves a hot hero, a heroine with attitude and a happy ending. Writing passionate stories for Harlequin Books is a dream come true. You can visit Lynn at www.lynnrayeharris.com.

Lynn Raye Harris

THE DEVIL'S HEART

TORONTO NEW YORK LONDON
AMSTERDAM PARIS SYDNEY HAMBURG
STOCKHOLM ATHENS TOKYO MILAN MADRID
PRAGUE WARSAW BUDAPEST AUCKLAND

Recycling programs
for this product may
not exist in your area.

ISBN-13: 978-0-373-12986-7

THE DEVIL'S HEART

First North American Publication 2011

Printed in U.S.A.

THE DEVIL'S HEART

To my agent, Karen Solem, whose awesome
advice and unwavering support are
so very much appreciated.
Thanks for everything.

PROLOGUE

Centuries-Old Missing Treasure Resurfaces

Washington, D.C.—Last night onboard his yacht anchored in the National Harbor, Massimo d'Oro hosted a party for his daughter. Francesca, the youngest child of the Italian businessman, celebrated her eighteenth birthday in a style to which lesser mortals can only dream. The party was attended by many of Washington's social elite, and the birthday girl's dress was rumored to have been custom designed by the House of Versace. The party is said to have cost Mr. d'Oro over one hundred thousand dollars.

Most spectacular of all was the gift Mr. d'Oro bestowed upon his daughter: a ninety-carat diamond necklace, the centerpiece of which is the fifty-five carat flawless yellow diamond known as *El Corazón del Diablo* (The Devil's Heart). This gem, once belonging to the Kings and Queens of Spain, was last known to have been in the possession of the Navarre family of Argentina; it has been lost since the 1980s.

CHAPTER ONE

Eight years later...

"I BEG YOUR pardon?" Marcos Navarre stared at the slight figure dressed in dark clothes. The gun pointed at his heart never wavered.

"I said *move.*"

This time the voice was less gruff. Marcos stepped away from the hotel room door, hands up just enough so this intruder wouldn't think he was about to do something crazy.

Like lunge for the gun.

If he could get close enough, he would do just that. This wasn't the first time he'd been on the business end of a weapon, and fear was not what motivated his seeming compliance. He'd become inured to violence during the years he'd spent living in South American jungles with a guerilla army. He knew without doubt there was always an opportunity, in situations like this, to gain the upper hand. So long as his hands were free, there was a chance.

No, fear was not at all what he felt. Rage was the word he was looking for. Bone deep rage.

The person facing him was small, though he knew

better than to mistake small for weak. Darkness shrouded the room and he couldn't make out any details about his visitor. But Marcos had several inches of height, and many more stones of weight to his advantage.

The moment he had an opportunity, he would act. The key was to remain free, and to keep his senses on high alert. He refused to consider what he would do should this intruder attempt to restrain him in any way. Memories flashed into his mind: a dark room, the sharp odor of sweat and rage, and the feel of his own blood dripping down his wrists.

No. Focus.

"You are wasting your time," Marcos said mildly. "I am not in the habit of keeping large amounts of cash in my room."

"Shut up."

Marcos blinked. The gruffness in his intruder's voice was gone. The person holding a gun on him so coolly was most definitely a woman. He relaxed infinitesimally.

Dios mío.

Who had he offended this time? Which of his ex-lovers was so incensed as to carry her desperation this far? Fiona? Cara? Leanne?

He was generous with his mistresses, yet there were those who refused to accept his decision to end the relationship when the time came. Was this a jilted lover— and why couldn't he place her immediately? He was not so callous as to ever forget a feminine body or voice when they gave him such pleasure.

No, not a jilted lover then. Unless he was growing forgetful. Marcos frowned. It did not seem likely. He'd had a lot on his mind lately, yes, but surely not so much as to render him incapable of remembering a woman he'd been intimate with.

He kept his hands in her sight, moving carefully into the middle of the room to await instruction. She shrank back when he passed by, then righted herself boldly as if irritated she had done so.

Several moments passed in complete silence but for the whisper of the ceiling fan overhead.

"Retrieve the jewel," she said, all pretence of being a man gone from her voice now. So she'd made a decision to give up that deception, had she?

Bueno. It would make it easier for him to learn her identity.

"I'm afraid I don't know what you're talking about."

She growled impatiently. The gun gleamed bluish in the moonlight shafting into the room. He noted that she'd added a silencer. The thought did not give him comfort.

"You know very well what I mean. The Corazón del Diablo. Bring it to me if you wish to live."

Ah, so now it made sense. He should have ignored the ridiculous claims of the d'Oros and refused to bring the jewel back to America. But his business interests here could suffer if he did not put an end to their fraudulent claims. The courts in Argentina had already ruled in his favor. He did not need an American court's approval to keep what was rightfully his. What he'd paid for in blood.

Had this woman been sent by the d'Oros? Was the lawsuit merely a ploy to get the stone back into the United States so they could steal it? The old man was dead, but the girls were still alive. He shoved aside the pang of regret he felt when he thought of the youngest d'Oro girl.

Why he should still feel regret, when she'd manipulated him as much as any of them, was a mystery.

Part of him insisted she was innocent—and part of him knew the dark depths to which the human soul could travel. Innocence was often a façade for treachery.

"If you shoot me, *querida*, you will never have the jewel."

"Maybe I'll have something far better," she spat in a low voice.

All of Marcos's senses went on high alert. Something about that voice…

Something he'd forgotten…

"I'll take that jewel now," she continued. "It's in the safe. Open it."

Fury began to uncoil within him. Who was this slip of a woman and how dare she try to rob him of his family birthright? She was not the first to attempt it, but she would not succeed.

It was after the jewel had been stolen, when he was only a boy, that the military *junta* imprisoned his parents. They never returned. They were, like so many thousands of others, among the *disappeared*, those souls who were taken away by the ruling party and killed before democracy was restored in later years.

He blamed his uncle far more than he did the diamond. If not for Federico Navarre's ambition and greed, life would have been far different. But the Corazón del Diablo was all he had left of his family, and he would allow no one to take it from him ever again.

"Apparently you have failed to think this through, little one."

She took a step forward, the gun rock-solid in her grip. And then, as if thinking better of it, she stopped, shook her head so slightly he wondered if he'd imagined the movement. "Shut up and open the safe. Now."

He stood stiffly for only a moment. "Very well."

If he were lucky, she'd get too close.

Marcos strode toward the wall that housed the safe. Sliding the wooden panel aside, he flipped the dial in annoyance. Right, left, right. The tumblers clicked into place and the door opened.

"Frankie," a voice hissed. *"Hurry."*

Marcos stilled, straining to pinpoint the source. It had sounded oddly small and disembodied.

"Frankie," it said again, louder this time.

"Shut up," the girl said. "I'm working on it."

Ah, a radio. She was using a two-way radio to communicate with someone outside this room. Odd—and a rather inept choice for a skilled thief. Yet another puzzle piece to consider.

"Step away from the safe," she ordered, the gun glinting as she used it to motion him away. "And keep your hands where I can see them."

Marcos backed away carefully, hands at shoulder height. The girl waited until he was nearly against the opposite wall before she moved. A flashlight blazed into life. She swept the interior of the safe, then spun toward him.

"It's not here," she said in disbelief. "Where is it?"

He almost felt sorry for her. Almost, but not quite. "There are plenty of other jewels. Take them instead."

Her voice shook. "The Corazón del Diablo. Where is it?"

"It's not here," he repeated.

"That's impossible. I was assured—" The gun was

leveled at him again, her voice full of purpose. "Where have you hidden it?"

"Forget it, *Frankie,*" he said smoothly, emphasizing the name the voice had called her. She had been assured? By whom? "You've failed. Now take what's there and go."

"You aren't the one in control here, Navarre. You will not tell me what to do. Not ever again," she added so quietly he wasn't certain he'd heard her right. *Never again?*

"Who are you?" he demanded, blazing hot anger sizzling through him like a living flame.

Before she could answer—or tell him to shut up, most likely—he reached over and flicked the light switch.

"Bastard," she cried, blinking against the light that flooded the room. Yet still the gun was firmly pointed at him.

He didn't care. The girl, this Frankie, was compelling—and he'd never seen her before in his life. Sun-streaked hair was pulled into a tight knot at the base of her neck, its thickness indicating long length when her hair was down. Her skin was pale with a hint of golden color. Her eyes glared at him hot and dark. She was dressed in a workman's black coveralls, but the garment was a size too small because it clung to her generous curves like a protective sleeve.

She looked furious, determined—but then she bit down on her plump lower lip and he recognized it for what it was: a crack in her armor. A current of desire arced through him at that single display of vulnerability.

Dios, now was not the time to be attracted to a woman. Especially not a woman with a gun pointed at his heart. Marcos clamped down on his wayward libido and tried to memorize everything about her. Should she get away, should she not shoot him in the process, he needed to remember what she looked like.

Because—female or not, vulnerable or not—he was going to hunt her down. He would find her and he would make her pay for thinking she could rob him of his birthright.

"Who are you, Frankie, and why do you want my necklace?"

Her eyes widened briefly before narrowing again. The gun shook in her grip. Odd when she'd been so controlled only moments before.

"You really don't know, do you?" Her laugh was strangled. "God, of course you don't. Because you're selfish, Marcos Navarre. Selfish and cruel."

Some little bit of knowledge buzzed at his mind like an annoying mosquito. He brushed it aside impatiently. He had no time to puzzle out what it was. He simply needed to remember this woman—and possibly disarm and capture her—before she could get away. "The Corazón del Diablo is mine. You will not steal it from me this night, so either take what's there and go, or shoot me and be done with it."

"I would like to," she said, her voice dripping with menace and fury. "Believe me I would. But I want that jewel, Navarre. One way or the other, you are going to give it to me."

Francesca forced down the bile in her throat. When he'd flipped the light on, she'd thought she would die. If he'd looked at her with pity, or shook his head sadly, she'd have crumbled like a house of cards. Her will and determination would have evaporated like an early morning mist, leaving her vulnerable and exposed.

But there'd been no flicker of recognition in his eyes, no stiffening of his form, nothing to indicate he had the slightest clue who she was.

And it hurt. Hurt like bloody hell that he hadn't known her. After all, she'd been the one to give him the Corazón del Diablo in the first place. Like a love struck imbecile, she'd handed it over just the same as she'd handed him her heart.

What happened next had been inevitable to all but the most blind of souls. He'd kept the jewel and discarded her love. Discarded her. She'd learned the truth too late. He'd conned her out of the diamond just like he'd conned her into believing he cared.

The Devil's Heart was aptly named. She'd given it to the devil and it had cost her nothing but heartache.

And now he stood here so haughty and handsome in his custom tuxedo, looking down his fine nose at her as if she were a bug. Her traitorous heart thumped painfully.

He was still so damn gorgeous. Tall, broad-shouldered, and as handsome as any movie star. He had a silver-edged scar that zigzagged from one corner of his mouth, a reminder of a long ago accident, she imagined. Far from ruining his dark male beauty, it only made it seem more potent. He had the kind of Latin good looks that made women prostrate themselves at his feet.

Just like she'd done. *Idiot.*

Her life had been ruined by that single act of falling for Marcos Navarre's smooth lies and sensual body. For thinking she had a future with him if only she gave him what he wanted. She'd been stupid. How could a man like him ever be interested in a chubby, shy, ugly girl like her?

He couldn't. Her sister had tried to warn her, but she hadn't listened. She'd believed Livia to be jealous. Livia, the beautiful one. The one who *should* have been the object of Marcos's attention. But Francesca hadn't wanted to accept the truth and she'd tumbled them into ruin with her need to be loved.

He'd fooled them all, she reminded herself. Charmed them all.

Didn't matter. It was *her* fault the Navarres destroyed d'Oro Shipping. Her fault that her father shot himself, that her mother clung to the remnants of her wealth in a drafty old house in Upstate New York, and that her sister barely ever spoke to her.

She'd made poor choices, choices that had cost her much more than hurt pride in the end.

She was through letting life beat her up and take away the people she loved. Her grip on the warm metal hardened.

Jacques was not going to die, not if she could help it. The old man had taken her in when she'd fled after her father's death, had given her a job and taught her everything he knew about the jewelry business. He'd also nursed her through the darkest moments of her life when she'd wanted to die, along with the child she'd never gotten to hold. After Marcos's betrayal, it had taken years to let a man into her life. Robert hadn't thrilled her the way Marcos had, but she'd told herself it was simply her youthful longings making Marcos seem so much bigger than life in her imagination.

Getting pregnant was an accident, but she'd wanted her baby as soon as she found out. Robert hadn't, though he'd stuck around for a few months, had even gone through with an engagement as if he were prepared to be a husband and father. Until she started to show. That's when he walked out.

When she lost the child so brutally, Jacques was the only one who cared, the only one who was there for her.

She loved Jacques and she owed him.

"The necklace, Marcos," she said firmly, leveling the gun at his heart once more. "I'll take it now."

"It's not here, *querida*. You waste your time."

Francesca lowered the gun to point at his groin. "Killing you would be too good. Perhaps I will simply have to deprive the female world of your ability to make love ever again. I am quite a good shot, I assure you."

She'd learned out of necessity. And though she never wanted to harm another human being, she had no compunction about making this man think she would do so if it meant she could save Jacques.

His voice dropped to a growl. A hateful, angry growl. "You won't get away with this. Whoever you are, *Frankie,* I will find you. I will find you and make you wish you'd never met me."

Her heart flipped in her chest. She ignored it. "I already wish that. Now give me the jewel before you lose the ability to ever have children."

Bitterness twisted inside her as she said those words. How ironic to threaten someone with something she would never wish on another soul. But she had to be hard, cold, ruthless—just like he was.

He stared at her in impotent fury, his jaw grinding, his beautiful black eyes flashing daggers at her. Very slowly, he reached up with one hand and slipped his bowtie free of its knot. Then he jerked it loose and let it fall.

Francesca forced herself to breathe normally as he undid the stud at his neck and his shirt fell open to reveal the hollow at the base of his throat.

"What are you doing? This is no time to attempt a seduction, Navarre," she said icily.

His fingers dipped into his snowy white shirt and came up with a silver chain. He tugged it upward, slipping it over his head and tossing it at her. Francesca caught it smoothly, though her heart thundered. She wasn't sure how she'd caught it when she'd barely seen him throw it.

The chain was warm from his skin, yet it burned into her as if it were on fire. She clenched it tightly, only realizing there was a key at the end of the chain when she felt it in her palm.

"What am I supposed to do with this?"

"There is a strongbox under the bed. The necklace is inside."

Too easy. He's up to something.

No, he simply cared about his balls more than he did the necklace. Typical. And exactly what she'd been counting on when she made the threat.

Francesca waved the gun. "Get it for me."

Marcos shrugged, then moved off toward the bedroom as if he hadn't a care in the world. She followed at a distance that kept her out of his reach if he were to turn suddenly. She put nothing past him. She hadn't known him well at all, still didn't, but she knew he was a dangerous man.

A devil wrapped in a beautiful package.

It's what had drawn her to him in the first place, the

danger of all that sharp, sensual, broody masculinity that hid the kind of dark secrets she hadn't begun to guess at in her sheltered life. That and the way he'd seemed to smile only for her.

Francesca suppressed a snort of disgust.

That naïve girl she'd been was gone. Buried in the past. The woman she was now knew all about secrets and pain.

She stopped in the doorway as Marcos moved toward the giant king-size bed that dominated the room. Silk sheets were turned down in anticipation of his arrival, and a silver bucket of champagne gleamed with sweat on the night table. Two crystal glasses sat beside the bucket.

Francesca clamped down on the rush of heat that flooded her limbs. Her ears grew hot. Of course he was expecting a woman. Wasn't he always expecting a woman?

She needed to get the necklace and get out before his paramour arrived. Another person would complicate matters. Perhaps that was what he was counting on—the arrival of a lover and the inevitable confusion that would follow.

"Hurry up," she said as he knelt beside the bed. "And don't try anything funny. I *will* shoot you, I swear."

He looked at her evenly. "Are you trying to convince me or yourself?"

Francesca gripped the gun harder. "Don't try me, Marcos. One handed," she added when he began to reach beneath the bed.

He kept one hand on the floor where she could see it and reached under the bed with the other. She heard the scrape of metal against the tile and then he emerged with a long black box.

"Now shove it over here and get on the bed," she said.

He stood to his full height and kicked the box with a vicious jab that sent it flying toward her. She stuck her foot out to stop it, wincing as it slammed into her.

"You can leave now," he said, his voice cold and deadly. "Leave the box and go, and I will not come after you."

"On the bed," she commanded.

One corner of his mouth suddenly crooked in a sensual grin. She didn't fool herself that he was anything other than angry. He was as alert as a panther, constantly looking for a way to catch her off guard.

"And here I thought you only wanted me for my jewels."

"On the bed, Marcos. Hurry."

"As you wish," he said. "Shall I strip first?"

When she didn't answer, he sat on the bed and eased back against the headboard. Francesca swallowed. God, he looked like a banquet of sinful delights as he leaned back casually, one knee bent. When he slipped open another stud, his shirt fell apart to reveal smooth, tanned skin that she'd once ached to kiss.

She'd never gotten to do so, but she'd wanted to desperately. And still he had no idea who she was. Incredible. She'd lost weight, but she hadn't changed that much. She was still Francesca d'Oro, as awkward and ungraceful as ever.

His inability to recognize her was yet another slice of proof, as if she needed more, that he'd never really been interested in *her*.

"Like what you see, *querida*?"

Francesca gave herself a mental shake, then reached into her pocket and withdrew a set of handcuffs. She tossed them at him. He caught them one handed, all pretense of seduction gone. His eyes gleamed with poorly disguised hatred.

And something else.

Was it fear she saw in the depths of his gaze? A tremor rolled over her, but she couldn't stop. She couldn't leave this room safely if he wasn't restrained. She tightened her grip on the gun, her sweaty palms making it harder to hold with each passing second. She had to get this done and get out.

"Cuff yourself to the bed. And make sure I hear the snap."

His grip on the stainless cuffs was white knuckled. "You really need to shoot me," he said evenly. "Because I will find you. And what I do to you when that happens will make your worst nightmare seem like a pleasant dream."

"Don't tempt me," she muttered. "Now do it."

He glared at her a moment longer, his chest rising and falling a little too quickly. But then he snapped one cuff to the bedpost. He fitted his wrist into the other cuff, his eyes hard on hers. She would almost swear his lips were white around the edges. But no, Marcos Navarre was afraid of nothing, certainly not of being handcuffed to a luxurious bed in a posh hotel. In fact, she would bet he'd been cuffed to beds before—though for infinitely more pleasurable reasons.

The cuff snapped in the stillness. For good measure, he jerked his arm against the restraints; they held fast and Francesca let out her breath.

Until he spoke.

"I will find you, Frankie. You will pay for this in ways you cannot imagine. I will start by binding you like a dog—"

"Shut up," she bit out, the gun wavering as she pointed it at him. But her heart pounded so hard it made her head feel light. He had no idea that she'd already suffered her worst nightmare. Nothing this man could do would ever equal what had been done to her when those thugs had beaten her half to death and killed her unborn child. "I don't want to hurt you, Marcos. But I will, I swear to God, if you force me to do so."

"Then open the box and retrieve your spoils," he said coldly. "Because I assure you we will meet again."

She bent to retrieve the strongbox at her feet, fumbling with the key as she did so. Adrenaline pumped into her veins, the rush of it heady and swift. Soon, she would have the Corazón del Diablo in her possession. Life would go back to normal again. Jacques would get well and keep making beautiful jewelry. She would continue running the small shop where they sold his creations.

A stab of fear pierced her. What if Marcos found her? But no, she couldn't worry about that possibility. Even if he did somehow remember who she was, and track her down, the necklace would be gone and Jacques would be getting the care he needed.

Not for the first time, doubt and guilt reared their ugly heads. Was it right to do this? But, oh God, what choice did she have? Marcos had wealth to spare. He would be fine without this necklace. Besides, he'd taken the diamond from her under false pretenses.

Do you promise to love, honor, and cherish....

A noise in the other room brought her head up.

"Darling, where are you?" a woman called, her soft voice accented with wealth and culture.

Francesca froze, her breath shortening in her chest. She'd had those things once upon a time. Things she'd lost, thanks to him.

No.

She'd never been happy in that life. In spite of all the culture and deportment lessons, she'd never been the kind of daughter her mother had wanted her to be. She wasn't perfect like Livia. Everything she'd ever touched, ever tried to do, crumbled apart like last winter's rotten leaves. Escaping had been a relief.

For a brief time, anyway. Until a new nightmare had nearly robbed her of her sanity.

"Darling?" the woman called again.

Francesca swung the gun up and motioned for Marcos to be quiet. Amazingly, he obeyed. She had no time to puzzle out why. She hefted the box and backed into the shadows of the open balcony. The last thing she saw as went over the side was Marcos Navarre's eyes.

They glittered hard and cold, promising retribution.

CHAPTER TWO

JACQUES LAY IN his bed, blankets pulled high, his frail body lost in the mass of covers. His eyes were closed, his breathing labored and shallow. Francesca swallowed a hard knot of pain. Her throat ached. She so badly wanted to tell Jacques about the jewel, wanted his help and advice.

But she couldn't. He would worry if he knew what she'd done. Across the bed from her, Jacques's nephew, Gilles, met her gaze. His eyes were shadowed. He'd helped her break into Marcos's room, and she'd felt the guilt of involving him each moment since.

And each moment since she'd left Marcos handcuffed to his bed, she'd felt tight inside, as if her skin were being stretched over a massive drum.

From the instant she'd seen the newspaper article that Marcos was bringing the Corazón del Diablo to New York, she'd thought of nothing else but regaining the stone. But now that she had, everything felt wrong. Though he'd stolen it from her in the first place, she couldn't stop thinking that she'd been dishonest in re-claiming the necklace the way she had.

Maybe she should have called Marcos, asked for a

meeting. Told him flat out it was hers and she wanted it back.

As if he would have listened! No, time was running out. For Jacques and for her. Livia and her mother had filed a suit claiming ownership. If they somehow won, or if the courts demanded Marcos turn the necklace over, she'd never see a cent.

She didn't have time to fight them all, nor did she have the money to do so. Perhaps she'd been wrong to steal it back, but she'd had no choice. Jacques was more important to her than a collection of polished carbon rocks and platinum.

She'd tried everything she could think of to get the money for his cancer treatments. No one would insure him with a pre-existing condition. She'd even called her mother to beg for money, though she should have known better. Penny Jameson d'Oro was no longer the fabulously wealthy socialite she'd once been. She had money, but to her it wasn't enough. She wouldn't part with a dime, and certainly not to the daughter she blamed for casting her into her current state of *poverty*—her word, not Francesca's—in the first place.

"Let me know when he wakes," Francesca said. Gilles nodded.

Francesca turned and made her way down the stairs to the shop. Thank God Gilles was here. The two of them took turns sitting with Jacques, and that enabled them to keep the shop going. Every bit of money they brought in was crucial.

She knew that if she wanted, Gilles would become more than just a friend. He was her age, strong and energetic, and he had a string of girlfriends he dated from time to time, though none seriously.

But she didn't want to cross that line with him, not really, even if she sometimes felt so empty and alone. Memories of Marcos sliding his shirt open and fishing for that key made heat curl in her veins.

Unwelcome heat.

She pushed the image away. Romance wasn't for her, and now was not the time to think about sexy Argentinians. She had to unload the Corazón del Diablo. Her stomach twisted.

You've come this far, she told herself. *Too late getting a conscience now.*

As soon as she opened the shop, she would make a few discreet calls.

The morning was gray and gloomy as she unlocked the doors. The air was beginning to turn brisk with the promise of winter. Yesterday, she hadn't seen her breath. This morning, it frosted and made her think about long ago days at her family's estate, when the leaves turned golden and the apple cider tasted spicy and sweet on her tongue.

She rarely thought of her life before, but seeing Marcos again dredged up memories of her past. She'd once daydreamed about what a life with him would be like, but he'd crushed her dreams beneath his custom soles. Life itself had dealt the final blow. She had no dreams left.

She went to the small kitchenette off the main showroom and poured a cup of coffee. The bell dinged in the shop, letting her know someone had come inside.

Cup in hand, smile fixed, she returned to the shop to help the first customer of the day.

A tall man stood with his back to her as he bent over a case. Outside the door, two more men stood with arms folded across massive chests. The hair on the back of her neck prickled in warning. The old horror threatened to consume her, but she wouldn't allow it.

Francesca set the coffee down quietly and slid her fingers toward the gun beneath the counter. They hadn't had a robbery attempt in months now, but she was taking no chances. Memories of pain and blood, of the fear she'd had for her baby as her assailant had kicked and punched her, flooded in as her fingers touched the cool metal. She'd learned to defend herself in the aftermath of that dark time, learned that she could be cold and calculating if lives depended on it.

"I wouldn't do that if I were you." The man turned toward her and all the breath left her lungs. She had an impression of cold, cruel strength. Of a strong jaw, tanned skin, and thick black hair.

And then he spoke again.

"*Buenos días*, Frankie. Or should I say Francesca?"

Marcos Navarre did not like being made a fool of by anyone. And a fool was what she'd tried to play him for. The woman looking back at him was nothing like the sweet, shy girl he'd once thought her to be. This woman was cold, hard, and ruthless. No wonder he hadn't recognized her.

At the moment she looked stunned, however. And maybe a touch vulnerable, though he dismissed the thought as fancifulness on his part. His protective instincts were too finely tuned, too accustomed to reacting to others' fear and pain. That's what a childhood in the streets of Buenos Aires did for a man.

He'd learned the hard way that he couldn't save everyone. Francesca d'Oro least of all. Oh yes, he'd had some misguided notion of rescuing her several years ago—when in fact she hadn't needed rescuing at all.

As she'd proved to him again just a few hours past.

He'd felt sorry for her once, had resented her a bit later—now, he hated her for what she'd done. She'd stolen the Corazón del Diablo from him, and she'd forced him to endure the kind of captivity he'd never thought to endure again. He hadn't spent long chained to the bed, but even a second was more than he cared to endure. He'd had to remember his darkest days, the blood and pain and fear as he'd been kept chained in a dark room and beaten for information all those years ago in the jungle.

Francesca couldn't have known what had happened to him—he'd never told her about it—but he hated her for her selfishness, for reminding him of what it felt like to be utterly helpless.

He was here to make her pay.

A noise on the stairs captured Francesca's attention before she'd recovered herself enough to speak. She took a step in that direction but was unable to halt the progress of the man who stumbled to a halt and stared at Marcos with barely disguised loathing.

"Please don't, Gilles," she said when the man looked ready to pounce on him. "It's not worth it."

The two exchanged a look and a different sort of rage blazed to life in Marcos's gut. The way this man looked at Francesca, the way they communicated without speaking another word. It was nothing to Marcos, and yet—

She turned back to him then. "Marcos—"

"Tell your lover who I am, Francesca. *What* I am to you."

There were two high spots of color in her cheeks. A moment later her expression hardened. "How dare you? You are *nothing* to me. Less than nothing."

"This is not what you said when you promised to love, honor, and obey me for the rest of our lives."

She didn't look at her lover, not once. She didn't have to. Marcos could tell the other man knew what their relationship had been. What manner of other things had she told him to get him to cooperate in stealing the necklace? Because Marcos knew this had been the man on the other end of the radio last night.

"We are *not* married, Marcos. Not any longer. You left, remember? And you did not contest the annulment."

He let his eyes move lazily down her body. Though she was dressed in a baggy black sweater and jeans, they did little to hide the lush curves underneath. Francesca d'Oro had not looked like this at eighteen. If she had, perhaps he'd have been unable to leave for Argentina so soon after their sham of a marriage had taken place.

She'd shed the baby fat that had once clung to her, rounding her face. The thick glasses were gone as well. Her hair had been blonde before, and cut in an unflattering bob that only made her face seem plumper.

Now, the golden-streaked mass was closer to brown than blonde and fell halfway down her back. Her eyes were hazel, he noted, more chocolate than green or gold, and her mouth was kissable in a way he hadn't remembered. Her lower lip was thicker than the upper, giving her an artless sexy pout.

He wanted to plunder that mouth, spend hours making love to it. The strength of the compulsion shocked him.

When he met her gaze again, he was almost amused

to see the hate in her eyes. If she thought she hated him before, she was certain to do so even more when he finished with her this time.

"I suggest you give me the Corazón del Diablo now, *querida*," he said coolly, twisting the endearment into an insult.

Her chin tilted up. "How did you find me so fast?"

He saw no reason to prevaricate. "You did not really think I would be so stupid as to trust that your family wouldn't pull a stunt such as this? There is a GPS transmitter attached to the necklace. These things are quite small now."

Her eyes closed briefly before snapping open to glare at him again. "It belongs to me, Marcos. You stole it on our wedding night."

"You gave it to me, *mi amor*. I remember this clearly."

"I would not have done so if I'd known you'd planned to abandon me."

"Ah yes, you thought I was bought and paid for, *sí*? That Daddy's money could bring anything your heart desired if only you begged him to buy it for you."

She flushed pink. "You're disgusting."

He shrugged casually, though anger scorched a path through his soul. Because he'd allowed himself to be bought, hadn't he? He'd wanted the Corazón del Diablo, had spent months attempting to purchase it from her father though he did not in truth have the money to do so.

But Massimo d'Oro was crafty. He'd given the jewel to his daughter. It was Marcos's fault for always paying attention to her. He'd believed she was a sweet girl, an ugly duckling who wilted in the shade of her more beautiful sister. Francesca had worn her innocence like a mantle, and he'd fallen for the act. He'd paid attention to her because she'd seemed to blossom when he did so. She smiled and came out of her shell and he only felt more protective.

Until the day her father had informed him that the only way to obtain the Corazón del Diablo—and his help in wresting control of Navarre Industries from Federico—was to marry Francesca. He'd realized then what he should have known all along: she was a d'Oro, vain, spoiled, and shallow, just like her mother and sister. Her gifts were not theirs; she hadn't been beautiful, so she'd had to use her other talents. And he'd fallen for it, just as they'd expected him to.

"You did not think I was so disgusting when you married me, *querida*." He sliced a hand through the air. What was done was done. "Enough of this reminiscing. You will bring me the Corazón del Diablo now or I will let my men tear this place apart looking for it. Decide."

Her answer was not what he expected, though perhaps he should have done so knowing what he did about her character.

"It's mine, Marcos. But I *will* sell it to you. For the right price."

Francesca wedged herself against the Bentley door and jerked the handle for the millionth time. She knew the result would be no different than before, but as furious as she was, she needed *something* to do.

Something besides launch herself at the man inside the car with her.

She'd already screamed until she was blue in the face. Marcos had threatened to gag her if she continued, so she'd stopped. In truth, her raw throat was relieved to have an excuse.

He had not reacted the way she'd expected. She hadn't really thought he would agree to pay her a dime, but she also hadn't believed he would kidnap her in broad daylight after he'd ordered his goons to search the store.

Furious tears pressed at the backs of her eyelids. Gilles had moved as if to prevent it from happening, but she'd begged him not to put himself in harm's way for her. He would have done so anyway, but one of Marcos's men pointed a gun at him and effectively ended the attempt. Gilles had stood by helplessly, fists clenching at his sides in impotent fury. She only hoped Jacques had slept through the raised voices and rhythmically slamming drawers.

What would happen when she was gone? How could Gilles keep the shop open and take care of Jacques too? Someone had to pick up Jacques's prescriptions, fix his favorite soup of clear broth and a little bit of egg noodles, and order the supplies for his bench. He didn't work often these days, but he still sculpted new creations out of wax when he felt up to it. When he finished a design, Gilles would cast it and start the rigorous polishing of the metal that was required before any gemstones could be set.

Oh, Jacques.

She crammed her fist against her mouth to stop the flood before it could break.

"Did you cry so prettily for me when we parted, Francesca?"

She swung her head around to look at him. "I'm not crying," she forced out between clenched teeth. The coolness on her cheeks betrayed the lie, but she refused to wipe the wetness away. She would not give him the satisfaction. "And I most definitely would never cry over you."

"Ah," he said. "How tragic for me then."

"Where are you taking me?"

His gaze grew sharp. "Buenos Aires, *mi amor.*"

Her heart began a staccato rhythm against her ribs. "What? You can't do that! This is my home, people need me—"

"I did warn you," he said, his voice deceptively mild and completely at odds with the fire in his gaze. She had the distinct impression he was enjoying himself.

"You don't want to do this."

"I do. Remember those words, Frankie?" He smoothed an imaginary wrinkle in his expensive sleeve.

"Stop toying with me, Marcos. And *don't* call me Frankie."

His dark eyes pierced her. "I thought you liked it. Is this your lover's pet name for you?"

Francesca wrapped her arms around her to ward off the chill creeping over her body. This man was nothing like the handsome young Argentinian who'd been so nice to her. But that had been a game, hadn't it? He'd only been nice to her in order to win her affection, to fool her into thinking he cared for her.

Once he'd gotten what he wanted, he'd left her to face the shame alone. He'd never even *kissed* her for God's sake! She'd been married to him for all of three hours and, aside from a peck on the cheek at the justice of the peace's office, they'd never shared a single kiss.

"You have to let me go," she said. "I can't be gone very long. Jacques needs me—"

"Ah yes, the man who owns the shop. Is he your lover too?"

She gaped at him, too shocked to summon outrage. "You went to all this trouble to find me, to find out who I was, and you didn't bother to learn that Jacques Fortier is seventy-five if he's a day, or that he'll die if I don't go back?" He looked so cold and unfeeling that a sob burst from her in spite of her best effort to prevent it. She stuffed the rest of them down deep before they could escape. "I need that necklace, Marcos. It's the only way to save Jacques. I need the money."

His mouth twisted. "A very likely story, Francesca. You forget that I know you, that I know what you are capable of. This Jacques may be sick, but he is simply the excuse you use to try and make me feel pity for you. You were always very good at that."

"No." She leaned toward him, tried to convey her sincerity, her desperation. "I'll go with you, I'll do whatever you want, I'll sign a paper saying I gave the necklace to you and that my mother and sister can have no claim to it. But you *must* help Jacques. Please."

He stared at her for so long she began to fear he hadn't heard her. "I have a better idea," he said, his voice so low she had to lean forward again. His gaze dropped and she realized that her baggy sweater was dipping perilously low, that he could see her bra and possibly the curve of her breasts.

As if her body could have any effect on him. No, she knew from experience that she did nothing for Marcos Navarre. She shifted position slightly, but only out of modesty. She could parade before him naked and he would not be affected.

"Anything," she said. "I'll do anything."

"Yes, I believe you would," he replied after another moment of letting his gaze wander.

Heat sizzled in the air between them. Her heart thumped, but she reminded herself it was only anger that charged the air, nothing more. What else could it be?

"You will come to Buenos Aires. Willingly, *querida*."

"I will," she replied quickly, though the thought filled her with dread. So long as he used his resources to help Jacques, she would dance naked on a tight rope if he demanded it. And yet she was curious. "Wouldn't a sworn statement to the authorities here be enough?"

"It might, but I prefer my solution. You will marry me—again—Francesca. Only this time, it will be a marriage in truth."

Her breath refused to fill her lungs properly. The blood rushed from her head, making her feel suddenly weightless. Of all the things she'd thought he would say, of all the things she would actually *do* to save Jacques, he'd chosen the one thing that would surely destroy her.

Marriage to him. Again.

"That's insane," she gasped. "I won't do it."

"Yet it is my price."

Francesca closed her eyes as she struggled to breathe normally. He had to be toying with her. This was part of his punishment for her, though she failed to see how it could possibly benefit him in any way. He was not attracted to her. Never had been. So what was the point?

Did he know about her ex-fiance? About her poor baby who'd been taken from her too soon? She hadn't been with a man since the miscarriage—was this his way of tormenting her? Did he really mean to marry her and bed her?

She'd said *anything* but she'd not considered this. The one thing that terrified her more than any other. She wasn't the naïve girl who'd once loved him, she wasn't in danger of losing her heart, but to be forced into intimacy with him when the act made her think of what she'd lost? Of what she could never have? Of the babies she would never, ever hold in her arms?

"You don't want me," she choked out. "You can't."

"Not permanently, no. I want you long enough to stop any claims to the Corazón del Diablo that your family might raise."

She had to find her center of calm, had to disconnect from the swirling emotion and deal with this situation as cold-bloodedly as he did. Her fingers shook as she clasped them together in her lap. She'd learned how to adapt, how to disconnect. She would do it here and now, in spite of how he churned her emotions. "How long, Marcos?"

He shrugged. "Three months, perhaps six."

Six months. Dear God.

She couldn't.

"I'll go with you. I'll sign papers stating the Corazón del Diablo is irrevocably yours, and I'll stay in Buenos Aires for three months if you'll help Jacques. But I can't marry you. There's no reason for it."

"There is every reason," he said, his voice cracking like a whip against her senses. "I will have no more questions about who owns the stone. It is mine by right, by birth. Any questions of ownership will be dead once we marry."

She felt like someone was squeezing her, sucking

all the air from her space. "How do I know you'll keep your word, that you'll help Jacques?"

"I'll put it in writing."

He was boxing her in and the box was growing smaller by the second. How could she refuse? How could she deny Jacques the same care he'd given her when she'd needed it? Comfort, care, and love. Francesca closed her eyes, swallowed.

"There would be no need for a marriage in anything more than name," she said, the words like razor blades in her throat. "You can continue seeing other women. When the time is up, we can divorce and no one will be the wiser."

The scar scissoring from one corner of his mouth made him look so dangerous, so sensual. When he smiled it made him look more predatory, not less. He truly was a devil.

"Ah, but I would know, Francesca." He grasped her hand, pulling it to his mouth. His breath stole over her skin in the instant before his lips seared her.

Her body reacted. God help her, it reacted. Sensation spread outward from that one hot touch of his lips. Flooded her senses. Brought parts of her to life that she'd thought were permanently shut off.

No! This was precisely why she couldn't do this.

You have to, Francesca. You have no choice.

"Stop touching me," she managed, her heart fluttering like a moth trapped in a jar.

His smile was still so wolfish. "I am not willing to 'see' other women, as you put it. I intend to be true to our vows, for as long as we are married."

He was torturing her. There was no other explanation. He didn't really want her—couldn't want her. But if she didn't agree to his plan, he wouldn't help Jacques. Uniting d'Oro and Navarre once more would cement his possession of the Corazón del Diablo in the eyes of the world. He would be satisfied with nothing less.

Once he'd done that, perhaps he would lose interest in punishing her. Perhaps he'd let her go.

Francesca pulled her hand away. "I want the contracts drawn up first. I want to see it in writing."

Marcos took out his phone and punched in a number. Moments later, he was speaking in rapid-fire Spanish. When he finished, he put the phone away and smiled again. That devastatingly handsome smile that proclaimed his intention to win no matter the cost.

"The contracts will be ready when we arrive."

"I'd rather see them before I leave New York."

"This is too bad," he said. "My plane is prepared and the flight plan has been filed."

"Flight plans can be changed," she insisted.

Marcos's eyes were hard. "Not mine."

"You can't force me to go with you," she said, throwing one last desperate statement into the air between them.

"I will carry you onboard myself, Francesca, if you insist on acting like a child."

"I'll scream until someone notices—"

"And sentence your Jacques to certain death? I think not."

"I hate you," she whispered, turning to watch the city slide by before he could see a tear fall.

His voice, when he finally spoke, was as soft as satin, as hard as the Corazón del Diablo. "Then perhaps we understand one another after all."

Francesca closed her eyes. She understood all right.
Understood that she'd just sold her soul to the devil.
And deals with the devil never ended well…

CHAPTER THREE

THE FLIGHT TO Buenos Aires took more than ten hours. Though they'd traveled in luxury aboard Navarre Industries' corporate jet, Francesca was exhausted by the time they arrived. She hadn't slept well since the night before when she'd stolen into Marcos's hotel room and liberated the Corazón del Diablo.

Though it was dark when they landed, the city lights bathed the night sky in a pale pink glow. Francesca stumbled on the stairs leading from the jet, but Marcos caught her around the waist and kept her from tumbling down the gangway. His fingers burned into her back as he guided her the rest of the way down.

A sleek Mercedes waited for them nearby. Francesca sank into the interior and moved as far away from Marcos as she could get. He immediately took out his phone and made a call. She listened to the lyrical sound of his voice speaking Spanish as the car left the airport and headed into the city. She spoke tolerable French and German, could read Latin, but she'd never learned Spanish. She was certainly regretting that now.

Marcos eventually finished his call and they rode in silence. The city moved by at a quick pace, but a few things caught her attention.

The obelisk that looked like the Washington Monument, which sat at the center of the very wide street down which they'd been traveling, for instance. When she remarked on it, Marcos informed her it was called *El Obelisco* and had been built to commemorate the four-hundredth anniversary of the city.

"There are concerts held here from time to time," he said, and she realized there was actually a semi-circular swath of grass and concrete on one side of the monument that could accommodate many people.

In fact, though it was dark, there were people everywhere, lingering around the obelisk or crossing the wide street. She even spotted a couple doing the tango. There was a crowd gathered to watch, but the scene slid by before she could see much of the dance.

In spite of her exhaustion, in spite of the reason she was here, the color and movement of the big city excited her. She'd traveled quite a bit as a child, but she'd never been to South America. Her mother had loved to frequent Paris, Rome, and the Med. While she and Livia fidgeted inside hotel suites with their tutors, her mother attended fashion shows and shopped like there was no tomorrow.

Perhaps her mother had been onto something, since most of her father's fortune died when he did. Penny Jameson d'Oro no longer took shopping trips abroad. A fact for which she firmly blamed Francesca.

"I don't believe I've ever seen a street so wide," she said in a rush, pushing away the ugly, depressing thoughts that came whenever she thought of her mother.

"No, you are not likely to do so either. This is the

Avenida 9 de Julio; it is the widest street in the world. There are twelve lanes of traffic."

"Fast traffic." Cars zipped along at Autobahn speed— or so it seemed.

"*Sí*, people are in a hurry to get where they are going."

"And where are we going? Is it much farther?" As much as she feared reaching their final destination, she also wanted to collapse on a bed and sleep for the next twelve hours.

"We are nearly there," he said. "My family home is in Recoleta."

"I thought we were in Buenos Aires. Have we left it behind?" It was entirely possible, she supposed. As tired as she was, they could have driven to another city and she wouldn't have really noticed.

"Recoleta is a *barrio*, a neighborhood."

"Did you grow up there?"

The corners of his mouth tightened, the scar whitening. "No. When my parents were taken, I was sent to live with relatives."

"Taken?" she said, zeroing in on that single word. Not *died*, not *left*, not *went away and never came back*. *Taken.*

"It is a long story, Francesca, and more appropriate for another night. Suffice it to say I have reclaimed the family home and moved back into it."

The car turned, and soon they were cruising along an avenue lined with ornate buildings that looked as if they'd been plucked from the streets of Paris and set down here. The architecture was ornate, beautiful, and decidedly French rather than Spanish. Soon they came to an iron gate that swung open on a mechanical hinge, then passed through and halted before an imposing white façade.

A lush collection of palm trees and flowering grasses grew in the little courtyard near the entrance. A man in a uniform hurried out to greet them as they stepped from the car.

"Señor Navarre, bienvenido."

"Thank you, Miguel. It's good to be home again."

A phalanx of men moved to the rear of the car and began removing luggage. Marcos ushered Francesca inside a grand entry hall with a giant crystal chandelier, black and white marble floor tiles set on the diagonal, and a huge Venetian mirror on one wall.

The elegance made her stomach flip. She hadn't been inside surroundings such as these in years. The weight of expectation threatened to crush her. Already she felt the walls closing in. She'd left deportment behind, left luxury and the expectation that went with it in the past. This place made her feel small, insignificant.

How could she do this now? How could she survive it? She would make mistakes, would fail where she should not. She wasn't cut out for this life, couldn't possibly masquerade as his wife for a single day, much less three—or six—months.

Marcos grasped her hand. Francesca uttered a little cry of surprise, then shivered when he lifted her hand to his lips and placed a kiss on the tender skin of her wrist. They'd spent the last several hours barely speaking to each other, and now this. It disconcerted her, flustered her.

What was he up to?

He gazed down at her, his expression a mixture of heat and hatred. It confused her, but not as much as his touch did. Why did she react? Why did she feel as if every cell of her body was straining toward him, wanting more?

"Until morning, *mi amor*. Juanita will show you to your room."

A young woman in a starched uniform stood nearby. She curtsied when Francesca looked over at her. Francesca gave her a weary smile, hoping she didn't look too wild eyed, before turning back to Marcos.

"Please don't call me that," she said in a low voice. She had to keep a distance between them, had to keep him from addling her with his sleek words and expert touch. She was still far too vulnerable to him, and it shocked her. She'd thought she'd left that girl in the past.

One dark eyebrow arched. "You do not like it? You would prefer *Frankie* now?"

Francesca pulled her hand away the instant his grip lightened. "No, of course not. But I don't want you calling me *your love* either. We both know I am not."

"*Sí*, we do indeed. And yet there is an appearance to maintain. We are marrying soon."

Francesca's heart skipped a beat. Dear God, what had she agreed to? She hadn't truly realized it until she'd walked into this…this *palace*.

Jacques, she told herself, she was doing it for Jacques.

"There's no reason to pretend we care for one another," she replied. Getting through the next few months would be hard enough. Pretending to feel things for this man was beyond her ability. She'd built a wall after he'd abandoned her so brutally; she didn't want to breach it ever again.

His expression grew hard. "There is every reason,

Francesca. As my wife, there will be many public duties you must perform. I won't have my reputation suffer simply because you are too spoiled to play the part you've agreed to. While you are here, while we are married, you will be *happy* to be my wife. *Comprendes?*"

Public duties. She would never pull it off. They'd know she was a fraud the instant she entered the room. And Marcos would not help Jacques.

She swayed on her feet before she could lock her knees. It was simply weariness and shock—fear, perhaps—that nearly made her fall. Marcos caught her, sweeping her into his arms and against his chest.

"No, please, it's all right," she managed. "Put me down."

He said something in Spanish, something low and dark, then barked out an order to the room in general before striding toward the curving staircase.

"I'm just tired," she said, hot embarrassment—and something else that contained heat—washing over her at the contact with his body.

She hadn't been this close to him when they were married, hadn't felt the power of his arms around her. But oh how she'd wanted to. How she'd dreamed of him sweeping her up just like this and carrying her into their bedroom while she laid her head against his shoulder and breathed in the wonderful scent of his aftershave.

Then he would lower her to the bed, whispering those words *mi amor*, before stripping her and kissing her and making love to her all night long.

But that was when she'd been eighteen. Now it was a nightmare to be so close to him. And to feel things she hadn't felt for a man in almost four years.

He strode up the steps and down a long hall while she

clung to him. The maid, Juanita, hurried past him at a run and threw open a door. Marcos carried Francesca inside and over to a low settee that stood beneath a tall window.

She closed her eyes as he set her down, both grateful and disappointed that he was no longer touching her.

When she opened them, Marcos stared down at her. "If you are pregnant with your lover's child, you had better tell me now."

She gaped at him, a sharp pain slashing into her heart. She felt like screaming, or laughing, or maybe even crying at the irony of the accusation, but she would do none of those things. She simply bit down on her lip and shook her head. "I'm not," she finally managed to force out. "I'm exhausted. I need sleep, not an inquisition."

"Perhaps you would not mind having blood drawn then. To verify."

Oh how she hated him in that moment. She had half a mind to tell him no, to ask if he'd care to take other medical tests, but she decided it wasn't worth the effort. It was a terrible invasion of her privacy, not to mention a hot dagger in her soul, but she only had to think of Jacques in a hospital, getting the best care money could buy.

"Draw all the blood you like. I have nothing to hide."

"You are shaking," he said, his brows drawing down as he studied her.

"I'll stop if you go away."

The tightness at the edges of his sensual mouth was back. The scar was white, and she knew she must have angered him.

Too bad, because he'd angered her. And hurt her.

"Please just go, Marcos," she said, holding onto the edges of her composure by a thread. "I don't want you here."

He towered over her, six-foot four-inches of angry Latin male. "You may spend this evening alone, remembering your lover, but tomorrow we begin to act like a happy couple. *Buenas noches, señorita. Hasta mañana.*"

Before she could say a word in reply, he strode out of the door and closed it behind him. The maid arrived a few moments later and drew her a hot bath in spite of her protestations that she could do it herself.

She hadn't planned to take a bath, yet she discovered when she sank into the fragrant water that she welcomed the chance to scrub away the chill that hadn't left her since Marcos had asked if she was pregnant.

Francesca closed her eyes as she leaned back on the bath pillow Juanita had provided. Damn him!

He was arrogant and proud, far more so than she remembered. She used to be in love with him, but it was a naïve, girlish love. The woman in her couldn't love a man like that.

She could want him, unfortunately, but she could never love him. Francesca tried to forget the way her body reacted when he'd held her. She'd melted, in spite of her anger. She'd wanted, for those few minutes he carried her, to be in his arms naked. To wrap her legs around his waist and feel the power of his body moving inside hers.

Oh God.

It was shocking to feel physical desire when she'd thought she would never do so again.

Francesca ran cold water into the bath to cool her heated imaginings, then climbed from the tub and dried off before she could start thinking of him again. She picked up the grey silk pajamas Juanita had left out for her. Briefly, she considered digging into the suitcase she'd hastily packed in search of her favorite cotton T-shirt, but the silk felt cool and soft, and it was so much easier to put them on than to search through her things for something familiar.

In spite of her exhaustion, she lay awake for what seemed like hours, listening to the strange sounds of a strange house and wishing she were back home in her tiny loft. She was just drifting off when a noise woke her.

A harsh cry. She bolted up in bed, her heart pounding. Had she imagined it?

But no, there it was again. A man's voice, hard and harsh and full of anguish. She shoved the covers off and padded toward the door. Could no one else hear him? Should she get someone? What was going on?

Francesca pulled open the door and peered into the hallway. There was nothing there, nothing but silence and moonlight. Another sound came from behind the door across the hall and her pulse shot higher.

Slowly, she crept toward the entry, arguing with herself the whole way. Whoever was behind that door needed help, didn't he? But maybe he didn't. Maybe he would be angry with her for intruding.

She reached for the handle, twisted it. But the door was locked. The voice cried out again and any reservations she had evaporated. He sounded as if he was in pain. She pounded on the door, calling out to whoever was inside.

The noise stopped abruptly. Another minute and the door was wrenched open. Marcos stood in the opening, a sweat-soaked T-shirt clinging to his skin.

Francesca took a step backwards at the wild look in his eyes. "I heard something," she said. "I-I—"

"You are quite safe here," he said harshly. "You need not worry about intruders."

She blinked. Was he deliberately misunderstanding her?

"I thought someone was hurt."

"No one is hurt." He looked weary for a moment, but then the hard façade was back and he seemed angry. "Go back to bed."

The door slammed in her face. Francesca stood there in the silent hallway, wondering if she'd imagined the entire thing, wondering if she should knock again and make sure he was all right.

Finally, she returned to her room. It was a long time before she drifted into a restless sleep.

Marcos lay on the floor, unwilling to return to the soaked sheets of his bed. He could call someone to change them, but he knew from experience that he would sleep just as well on the floor as on the bed. The hard floor reminded him of what it was like to sleep in the jungle. Or on the street.

He hadn't had nightmares this bad in quite some time. Lately, however, he seemed to experience them more frequently. Being cuffed to the bed in the hotel hadn't helped, even if it had been of relatively short duration in comparison to his time in the enemy's prison.

Regardless, the experience brought back the flood of

memories and turned him once more into the kind of animal whose sole focus was survival.

He thought of Francesca standing in the hallway, of her wide eyes and tousled hair, and felt a mixture of hate and desire so strong it frightened him. When he'd jerked the door open, he'd wanted to haul her inside, strip her naked, and lose himself in her body for a few hours. It had taken all his willpower not to do so.

He'd also wanted to lash out, to bind her to him and make her pay for dredging up the memories of his past. Not for the first time, he wondered if bringing her here had been a mistake. Perhaps he should have simply taken the jewel and returned to Argentina. But she was here now, and he was committed to the course of action he'd chosen.

Marcos would allow nothing—and no one—to ruin all he'd worked for. And he would survive his nightmares. He always did.

"Spanish lessons? Is this necessary?" Francesca blinked at the calendar Marcos had handed to her. It was filled with appointments. Spanish lessons, culture lessons, tango lessons, shopping, hair, nails…

It was already late morning. After the night she'd had, she'd slept in far longer than usual. She'd showered and dressed in a pale blue peasant blouse and white jeans, one of the best outfits she owned these days. She'd wondered if Marcos would be here, or if he would be gone to an office for the day. She'd hoped he would be gone, because she didn't know what to say to him after last night.

She still didn't.

Marcos looked implacable as she met his gaze once

more. He also looked delicious, in spite of the restless night he must have had. His dark good looks were only enhanced by the white shirt and casual chinos he'd selected today. His shirtsleeves were rolled loosely, revealing his forearms. Powerful forearms.

One of them bore a crude tattoo of what she thought might be crossed swords. The ink bled at the edges, blurring the design. She didn't remember that from eight years ago, but had she ever seen him in short sleeves?

Possibly not.

"You do not speak Spanish," he said. "It is necessary."

Francesca tore her gaze from his tattoo. "But I'm not going to be here very long, so why bother?"

Marcos shrugged. "Why bother doing anything, Francesca? Why get up in the morning to watch a sunrise, why eat ice cream, why read a book, why take a walk on the beach? Because they are worth doing, that's why. Just as learning Spanish, for as long as you are here, is worth doing. Think of it as an adventure."

"I don't like adventures," she replied. "I like everything the way I expect it to be, and I like my life the way it is. *Was*."

"Yes, I seem to remember you were always a scared little rabbit."

Embarrassment wrapped a hand around her throat and squeezed. "I was shy."

He snorted in disbelief. "That's an old excuse. Don't try to hide behind it."

"I'm not hiding behind anything. And I know what I want. Don't try to analyze me, Marcos."

He shoved his hands in his pockets, his sleeve dropping to cover the tattoo when he did so. "It is an observation, not an analysis."

"So why do you have that tattoo?" she asked. Anything to deflect the conversation away from herself. Away from her shortcomings.

He lifted his arm until the sleeve fell away. She stared at the green-blue ink, suddenly unsure she wanted the answer. Especially if it had anything to do with the sounds he had made last night.

"I did not choose it," he said. "But it was necessary. Necessary to prove I was loyal."

"Loyal to what?"

His eyes burned into hers. "You don't want to know."

She swallowed. "Maybe I do. Does it have anything to do with your nightmares?"

If she'd expected a reaction, she didn't get it. Instead, he closed the distance between them, reached out to tilt her chin up with a finger. "Nice try, *querida*. But it won't work. Your first Spanish lesson is in an hour."

Her skin sizzled where he touched. "Do you keep it to remind you of something? Because they can laser those off, you know."

His finger dropped away, his gaze shuttering. "It is my own business, Francesca."

She stared at him for a moment before clearing her throat and gazing at the calendar again. "Surely I don't need to learn the tango."

"It is the national dance of Argentina."

"And two-stepping to country music is rather popular in America. I don't remember you attempting to learn this when we married before."

"The two-step is hardly a national dance, and you

are only half-American." His brow furrowed. "Come to think of it, I never saw you dance in all the months I knew you."

"I don't like to dance."

It wasn't true, but she'd always seemed to have two left feet when she'd gone to ballet classes. Livia flourished while Francesca stumbled. She'd been too fat to get her leg up on the bar, a fact which her mother took so seriously she ordered Francesca be fed a diet of lean chicken, fruit and rice until she could achieve the feat. It took two months, but she had got her foot on that bar. And she'd kept it there, even if she was graceless in every other way.

Marcos raked a hand through his hair. "Then you will learn. It is expected that my wife will be able to tango."

His wife. The words gave her chills. And another feeling she didn't dare analyze. "I don't seem to remember this was a requirement before. And I've yet to see a contract, so this talk of what I must do as your wife is rather moot at the moment."

"The contract will arrive soon. And *I* don't seem to remember having much of a say in anything to do with our marriage before." The look he gave her was loaded with suppressed fury.

Her ears burned hot. She'd been too young and starstruck to question her good fortune when they'd married. She'd thought it was real, fool that she was. "That's not my fault."

"Isn't it? I was nice to you, and you thought that gave you the right to have me for your own." He swore in Spanish. "You sent your daddy to buy me like I was a prized pony, Francesca. Don't pretend otherwise."

Sudden fury burned through her bones, leaving hot ash in its wake. She was tired of taking the blame for their sham of a marriage and the consequences it had wrought on so many lives. Suspicion went both ways, whether he realized it or not.

"*Why* were you nice to me, Marcos? Did you hope my father would agree to let you marry me? That the Corazón del Diablo would be yours because I was young and stupid and loved you blindly?"

He took a step toward her. "How dare you try to turn this around? *You* were spoiled, selfish, a d'Oro female accustomed to getting what she wanted. And you wanted me. Nothing could have stopped you—and I was fool enough to fall for your shy and innocent act."

He thought she was like her mother? Like Livia? She would laugh if it didn't hurt so much. He'd never known her at all. Everything she'd believed about him had been a lie. She'd known it for a long time now, but to have to relive it opened old wounds.

Francesca jabbed a finger into his chest. "There was no reason for a man like you to be nice to me. I was nothing, *less* than nothing to you. I wasn't capable of attracting a busboy's attention, let alone yours, so you were only nice to me for one reason. You *wanted* me to fall for you. It was part of your plan all along."

He made a sound in his throat very like a growl. "You did not possess the necklace when I first met you. Your father had it, though he would not admit it. And I was nice to you *then,* before you ever possessed it, because I felt sorry for you."

Francesca drew in a sharp breath. Of course she'd known he'd felt sorry for her. Of course.

So why did it hurt to hear him say it?

Because he'd ruined the fantasy, the slim hope she'd harbored that it was something about her, something he saw that no one else did. He felt sorry for her, nothing more. She turned away from him, more affected by the admission than she cared to admit. It was years ago. Over and done with. Why did it matter? She'd certainly dealt with far worse blows to her ego since then.

Far worse.

She drew in a fortifying breath and turned back to him. Her lip trembled; she bit down on it. "There was a lot to feel sorry for, wasn't there? Forty extra pounds of it."

His face was a thundercloud. "Weight is not important."

She laughed. "Oh yes, of course it's not. That woman in your hotel suite didn't have an ounce of extra fat, nor have the models and actresses you are usually photographed with. Well, rest assured Marcos, I will endeavor not to embarrass you by asking for second helpings at the dinner table."

"A woman's weight is only important to her," he said. "If she is comfortable in her skin, then weight is unimportant."

"God you're a hypocrite." Anger rolled through her in a fresh wave. "You never even kissed me. We were married and you never kissed me properly because I disgusted you."

"I never kissed you because I was angry." He took a step closer, looming over her. "I'm still angry. But I should have kissed you. I should have taken everything you offered."

Francesca took a step backward, her breath catching at the look in his eyes. She'd challenged him—and he wasn't about to back down. "I don't know what you're up to, but don't you dare kiss me now. It's too late for that."

"It's never too late," he said, yanking her close. Before she could process the million and one sensations of finding herself pressed to him so intimately, he dipped his head and claimed her mouth for his own.

CHAPTER FOUR

FRANCESCA TRIED TO pull out of his grip, but it was like trying to bend an iron bar. Her heart pounded so hard she thought surely he could feel it in his bones. One broad hand rested against the small of her spine, pressing her into his hard body. The other threaded into her hair, angling her head back to give him better access.

His tongue plunged between her lips. She'd meant to rebuff him. Meant to shove him away and refuse to engage in the kiss.

But being kissed by Marcos Navarre was a sensual bombardment. She could hardly remember her name, much less the fact that she was supposed to resist.

The kiss was thrilling. Arousing. Delicious.

She'd dreamed of kissing him when she was a girl. Dreamed of how sweet and tender it would be. Of how he would take her hand, look deeply into her eyes as he pulled her closer. Of how his head would dip, his eyes closing gently while her heart slammed into her ribs and she stretched up to meet him.

This kiss, however, was not sweet or tender. It was raw, untamed, and threatened to incinerate her from the inside out.

This was the kind of kiss a man gave a woman. The kind of kiss that said *I want you* and *You are mine*.

But why? Why would he kiss *her* like this? She wasn't the sort of woman he preferred, wasn't soft and gorgeous and oozing femininity. She'd desperately wanted to be when she was eighteen, yet she'd always known deep inside that he was not attracted to her. He could not be so now, either. It was a ploy, a means of subduing her.

And, God help her, it was working.

She'd pressed her hands to his chest to push him away, but now they lay against the soft cotton of his shirt, useless. Her body was softening in places she'd thought long dead. Melting. Liquefying.

When was the last time she'd felt sexual desire?

Over four years ago.

She'd had a few lovers over the years, and she'd enjoyed sex well enough. But after Robert abandoned her, after her baby was taken from her so tragically, she'd lost all desire for a man.

Until now.

Why, dear God, did it have to be this man?

Marcos's hand skimmed up her side, over the swell of her breast. She couldn't stop the little moan that escaped her when his thumb brushed her nipple. *So long since she'd felt pleasure...*

She leaned into him, on the verge of losing herself in his heat and maleness. Just once. Just this once, she wanted to feel alive again...

But what was she doing? If she allowed this, she was no different than the naïve girl she used to be, the girl who would have done *anything* to be what he desired. That girl was dead and buried, along with her innocent belief in unconditional love and all-consuming passion.

Francesca gripped his wrists, intending to push his hands away. But his body went rigid. He broke the kiss abruptly, jerking his arms from her hold so viciously that her fingers stung where he'd ripped her grip apart.

He was breathing hard, that haunted, wild look in his eyes again. The same look as last night.

"Marcos, what's wrong?"

He shook his head, shoved a hand through his hair as he put distance between them. "It's nothing. Forget it."

"It didn't feel like nothing." Was it because he'd realized who he was kissing? That he could no longer keep his disgust under control? She wrapped her arms around her chilled body. Of course that was it. She repulsed him.

And suddenly that angered her, especially after the way she'd responded to him. He made her feel things she'd thought forgotten—and she made him feel disgust.

"I told you not to kiss me. If you knew you would find the experience so repulsive, you shouldn't have done it."

"And I told you to forget it," he growled.

"I've been trying to forget for the past eight years," she said. "I was doing a pretty good job of it until you dragged me here."

He looked utterly furious. "Had you not tried to steal the Corazón del Diablo, you wouldn't be here. Do not blame me for your actions."

"You stole it first, Marcos. Or have you forgotten?"

"You have no idea what you are talking about,

Francesca," he bit out. "That gem was stolen from my family. It was never yours to begin with."

She clenched her fists at her side. "If you're saying that my father stole it—"

"No, my uncle did. And he used it to entice your father into business with him. But it wasn't his to give."

She stared at him, momentarily at a loss for words. She'd never heard this much of the story before. She'd only known that the Corazón del Diablo had once been in the Navarre family. She'd thought her father had bought it, like he'd bought so many other things he'd wanted. And when she'd married a Navarre, she'd thought he would be happy if she placed the necklace in his hands, if it became a symbol of their union. She hadn't expected him to take the jewel and discard her. The memory of her naiveté still stung.

"Why should I believe you?"

"I don't care if you believe me or not. This is the truth, and the jewel is mine. By right, by birth, by long-standing tradition. It is not and never has been yours."

She didn't want to believe him—and yet she remembered that her father had refused to use the courts to try and recover the necklace. She hadn't understood at the time. Nor had her mother, who'd raged and cried and blamed Francesca for their misfortune.

And then…

"My father shot himself over it," she said numbly. "His business interests were tangled with Navarre Industries, and when your uncle went down, he did too. Without the necklace, there was no way to save the business."

His expression changed. "I know, and I'm sorry for that, Francesca."

She dashed away a tear. "Yes, well, that helps so much." He couldn't miss the sarcasm in her voice—and she didn't care. Let him know what his selfishness had cost. What it still cost. She'd never been particularly close to her mother, but at least she'd had a mother. Now, she no longer had that relationship. Nor did she have one with her sister, who followed their mother's lead in everything.

Francesca had been alone since the moment her dad had pulled the trigger. Which he never would have done had she not been so blinded by love that she'd given the Corazón del Diablo to this man. This devil.

"It was an unfortunate tragedy," he said, "but the jewel would not have saved him. He would not have been able to sell it, Francesca. Legally, he had no right."

She hated thinking about that time, hated thinking about the desperation and despair her father must have felt in those moments before he'd pulled the trigger. How different would it have been if she'd never married Marcos? But, if he was right, when the business went sour, her father still would have been broke. The Corazón del Diablo would have been about as useful as a paperweight.

"Then why didn't you just take us to court over it? If your claim was so great, why didn't you get a lawyer and sue?"

"Because I couldn't afford it," he said. "I hoped your father would do the right thing and return it to me. Instead, he gave it to you and told me the only way to get it was to marry you."

She couldn't help the bubble of hysterical laughter that erupted from her throat. Her poor, misguided father.

Always trying to make her happy, to even out the inequality between her and Livia. "Oh yes, and you had no trouble doing that, did you? Marry the ugly duckling and seduce the necklace away. Except you forgot the seduction part."

"You weren't ugly," he said, his voice low and hard. "And you know it. Eight years later, and still you try to use that act on me. It does you no credit, Francesca, not now. You are a beautiful woman, not an awkward girl."

She gaped at him, her heart thudding for an entirely different reason now. But she would not fall for his smooth words, not ever again. He would say anything to make this process as smooth as possible for himself.

"Don't you dare say those things to me, not when you don't mean them. I'm here, and you have the stone. I've also agreed to marry you so you can rest easy at night that a collection of damn *rocks* is all yours. So save the sweet talk for your mistresses."

Marcos gave a snort of disgust as he picked up a briefcase from a chair. "*Dios*, why bother? I have work to do. I'll send someone for you when the contract arrives."

Francesca wanted to throw something at his departing back, but the only thing in her hand was the calendar. And that simply floated to the floor with an impotent sigh.

The contract was every bit as humiliating a document as she'd supposed it would be. It was thick, typed on expensive paper, and bound in a slim leather cover. Francesca read it carefully while Marcos's lawyers explained the clauses in detail.

They were in his office, a surprisingly bright room

with a mahogany desk, built-in bookshelves, and sleek contemporary furniture. She sat on one of the low couches, a lawyer beside her, while Marcos leaned against the wall, hands shoved in his pockets, resembling nothing so much as a dark cloud as he frowned over the procedure.

It was all spelled out in excruciating detail, as she'd known it would be. Marcos had not reached the pinnacle of success he currently enjoyed by leaving anything to chance. They would marry for a period of at least three months, possibly more. She would relinquish, on behalf of her family, all further claims on the Corazón del Diablo forever.

And good riddance, she thought. The fiery stone at the heart of the necklace truly was the devil's heart. It had caused her nothing but trouble from the moment she'd possessed it. She had no wish to do so ever again.

Money. Her heart stammered over the clause about money. She had to work to keep her eyes on the page instead of looking up at Marcos. Did he expect her to be grateful? Or perhaps he expected a protest that it wasn't enough.

At the conclusion of their marriage, he would endow her with ten million dollars. It was a small sum to him, she knew, and yet it was enough to keep Jacques comfortable for the rest of his life. No doubt Marcos did it to keep her from making larger claims on his fortune, but to her it was an incredible sum after these last several years.

She hadn't expected it, and she certainly didn't want it. But she had to take it for Jacques's sake. Indeed, if not for Jacques and the way this money would enable her to take care of him, she would refuse to accept even a dime from Marcos Navarre.

She flipped the page, scanning for the most important part. When she found it, relief surged through her. Jacques's medical expenses were covered one hundred percent, no matter the cost. Francesca's eyes flooded with tears. She blinked them back, scanning the legalese for a trick or a condition.

There was none, other than the agreement to wed and be Marcos's hostess, bedmate, and partner for the duration of the marriage. Her heart thumped at that, but it was the price she had to pay to take care of Jacques. She would not fail him.

"Give me a pen," she said, cutting off the man on her right in mid-explanation. He reached into his suit jacket, but Marcos was there first, handing her an expensive, custom-made pen. She touched it to the paper and smoothly signed her name.

Just like signing a deal with the devil.

Marcos took the folder, laid it on the desk and signed, then closed it and handed it to the waiting lawyers. The two men departed, and they were alone. Humiliation was a strong brew in her veins, but it was the price she had to pay—and at least it would be of short duration in the scheme of things.

"I'm glad that's over," she said, tilting her chin up. "It was clever of you to put that part in about the marriage being consummated. No one will ever question the validity of it now."

Marcos studied her with that peculiar mixture of heat and hate she was accustomed to. Though perhaps there was less hate this time? But, no, surely she only imagined it.

"And what if I intend to follow the contract to the letter?" he said, his voice as smooth and silky as polished glass.

Francesca managed to shrug, though her heart sped up at the thought. "Then I suppose I agreed to it."

"*Sí*, you did indeed."

She pushed to her feet. She wanted to get away from him, wanted to go into another room and try to forget the way he made her heart pound simply by looking at her. "If you are finished with me, I believe I have a tango lesson to attend."

"Not this afternoon. We have another matter to attend to."

"And what is so important it takes precedence over the tango?" she asked as sarcastically as possible.

His mouth curved in a smile. An impossibly devilish smile. Her sense of foreboding rocketed into high alert.

"Our wedding, *mi amor*."

CHAPTER FIVE

MARCOS SUPPOSED HE should be offended, and yet he found that he was mostly amused. He should still be angry, but everything was going his way and that pleased him.

Francesca clearly did not feel the same. She flashed him a look of pure loathing as he helped her from the limousine that had taken them to the Civil Registry Office. It was rather like a kitten trying to imitate a tiger. She simply couldn't pull it off, no matter how she tried.

And he found it amusing, though he wasn't quite certain why.

She smoothed the fabric of the peach silk dress she wore. When she'd come down the stairs in this garment that set off the tawny gold of her hair, he'd been glad she hadn't chosen to wear white. This color suited her so much more appropriately than white or cream would have done. The only problem was in the cut of the dress. It was shapeless, as if she feared to show her curves. He would need to make sure something was done about that, he decided.

"I'm surprised you didn't wear black," he murmured as she accepted his arm and they turned to walk into the building.

"I wanted to, but I somehow failed to pack a black dress in the fifteen minutes you gave me back in New York."

Marcos chuckled. "So prickly on your wedding day."

She did not join in his amusement. "It didn't work out the first time, Marcos. I'm not expecting a vastly different experience the second time. And how did you manage this so quickly? I had read there are no quickie marriages in Argentina."

"I have influence, *querida*. Money is a powerful motivator."

"Lucky me."

"Lucky you indeed," he said. "If not for my money, your Jacques would not be receiving the treatment he so badly needs."

Marcos still hadn't puzzled out why the old man meant so much to her. He'd asked for a report on her life since he'd last seen her on their wedding night eight years ago, but the information he'd received was sketchy. Shortly after her father had committed suicide, she'd left home for good. She'd gone to work for Jacques Fortier in his small jewelry shop and led an unremarkable life.

A life quite different from how she'd grown up. It made no sense to him, but he'd made enough odd choices of his own over the course of his thirty-four years not to question too deeply why others did the same.

Now she stopped inside the door and turned to him. Her hazel eyes were golden today, shining with moisture. Surprise rocked him. She was on the verge of tears? But for what? Jacques Fortier? Or the inevitability of this marriage?

"I am grateful for your help, Marcos. For Jacques. In

spite of your reasons, or this marriage, or anything else, I am grateful you've gotten the best treatment for him. It's more than I'd hoped, truly." She laughed, the sound nearly breaking on a sob. She pinched the bridge of her nose. "God, I wasn't going to do this. Not today."

The sound was so plaintive he felt his heart constrict in sympathy. He skimmed a knuckle along her cheek because he could not stifle the impulse to do so. "I am not as cruel as you believe me to be, Francesca. No one should die because they cannot afford medical treatment. Jacques is lucky to have you fighting for him."

"But if I hadn't taken the Corazón del Diablo, we wouldn't be here and—"

"These things happen for mysterious reasons." He'd learned that particular truth on the streets and in the jungle. Sometimes there was no explanation for why things occurred as they did. Why good people suffered. Why children died.

Dios. There were things he didn't want to remember either, not now.

She looked up at him. "Why do you have to be nice?"

Nice? He hadn't quite thought of it that way, but if she did, he wouldn't disabuse her of the notion. "I can cease this niceness if it pleases you."

"Oh no," she said, shaking her head slightly. "I want to see how long you can keep it up."

"All night if necessary."

She dropped her gaze, as if she were uncomfortable suddenly.

He tilted her chin up, forced her to look at him. "There is no need to pretend with me, Francesca."

Tears glittered on her lashes like diamonds. He had to stifle the urge to kiss them away.

"I'm not pretending anything, Marcos."

"Do you really expect me to believe you aren't aware of how lovely you are?"

Her eyes widened, her smooth skin flushing pink. For the first time, he began to wonder if he was wrong, if she truly did believe she was still the awkward girl she used to be. Or maybe she was just manipulating him, trying to make him feel sympathy.

"Don't," she managed, her voice thready.

"As you wish, *mi amor*." He dropped his hand away and she took a deep breath. Collected herself once more.

She'd grown tough in a way she'd not been when he'd first known her. It made him wonder what, besides her father's tragic death and her family's loss of status, had happened to make her this way.

Perhaps it was nothing. Perhaps she'd simply grown cynical with the passage of years.

"Will anyone from your family be here?" she asked.

"No. Magdalena and her husband are staying at their winery in Mendoza. They could not get away."

"Magdalena is your sister, right?"

"*Sí*, she is my younger sister. She has just had her third child and could not get away."

Francesca's eyes dropped and she swallowed. Her knuckles, he noticed, were white where she clasped her hands together. "I see."

"You will meet her soon enough. We must go to Mendoza for a visit now that the baby is here."

If he'd thought that statement would soothe her, he was surprised to see that it seemed to have the opposite effect. She seemed agitated. And she did everything in her power not to look at him again. Her throat worked, as if she were swallowing back tears.

"You are afraid to meet my sister?" he asked.

She looked up again. "No, not at all. But what's the point, Marcos? This marriage will be over soon. Why introduce me to your family, make them think this is real when we both know it's not?"

"It would be odd if I did not, Francesca. Surely you can get through a few hours with them. No one will become so attached to you that they will be devastated once we divorce. It's a simple visit. And Magdalena will be far more focused on her new baby than on us, I can assure you."

"Of course," she said, her head dipping, her voice flat and emotionless. "If that's what you want, I suppose I have no choice but to comply."

She was married. Again. The ritual had been quick, sterile. Say a few words, repeat in the appropriate places, and then Marcos slipped a ring on her finger and brushed his lips against her cheek.

The office staff offered their congratulations before Marcos ushered her from the building and back into the limousine.

Francesca stared at the three-carat rock on her finger and felt numb. It wasn't as large as she'd expected, yet it was the perfect size for her. She wouldn't have wanted anything bigger, and though Marcos hadn't asked her opinion, he'd still managed to pick the ideal ring for her.

Odd to think it wasn't real, this marriage. Or that the perfect ring was only temporary. A Band-Aid to shield a wound, nothing more.

The stone shot fire as the light reflected off its facets. The platinum band was inset with diamonds. The matching wedding band was also diamond-encrusted. Though Francesca wouldn't tell a soul, she loved beautiful things. Always had, which is why her inability to please her mother with her looks and minimal grace had hurt so much. Francesca had wanted the beautiful clothes that Livia wore so elegantly. She'd wanted the jewelry, the poise, and the grace to match.

Though she was older and far wiser now, she still felt like the awkward teenager beside Marcos's smooth elegance. She hadn't worried over her looks in years, had thought they were perfectly adequate for the life she led with Jacques—but Marcos's arrival in her life had turned everything upside down again. He'd said she was lovely. But did he really mean it?

She shoved the thought aside brutally. She did not care what Marcos Navarre thought of her. Not any longer. The girl who'd desperately wanted his approval was buried in the past.

Marcos sat beside her now, his voice musical in her ears as he conducted business on his cell phone while they rode back to his home in Recoleta. *Their home.*

No, as beautiful as the French-style mansion was, it would never be her home. She was a temporary resident only, and she would not grow attached to the beauty of the place, the serenity of the cool courtyards with their fountains and thick foliage. She had a home in New York, with Jacques, and she would return to it as soon as Marcos let her go.

She prayed it would be sooner rather than later, but she knew Marcos was determined to fulfill some agenda that only he knew. And so long as he held the keys to Jacques's treatment, she would remain.

The visit to his sister would surely test her in ways she dreaded. She'd not been around babies since she'd lost her own. She refused to hold them, to play with them, to spend time with them. It wasn't that she didn't love babies; it was simply that being around them made her ache for what could never be.

Once, long ago, she'd thought Marcos would be the father of her children. But even if they'd married for love this time, that was impossible.

How would she survive being around a woman with a newborn?

One day at a time, Francesca.

It's how life was lived, how she'd survived the worst of the dark days in her past. One damn day at a time.

"We are attending a reception tonight," Marcos said smoothly as he tucked his phone away.

Francesca struggled to concentrate on what he was saying. She felt like she was being ripped apart inside, and he was informing her about a social event?

God help her.

"You will wear the Corazón del Diablo," he continued.

"I'd rather not."

His expression grew chilly. "Reneging already, Francesca?"

"The necklace is yours, Marcos. I see little point in asking me to wear it."

The idea of donning the necklace now, after all it had cost her, seemed completely foreign. And unnecessary. She had no doubt he knew it. He simply wanted to prove his mastery of her.

"I don't believe I asked," he said, his voice as smooth as aged whiskey. "You will wear it because it is mine, because you are mine."

Francesca drew herself up, her emotions whipping higher. "You don't own me, Marcos. You bought my cooperation, not me."

"You are still very foolish, aren't you?" he said softly.

Francesca felt the burn of anger—and the heat of embarrassment—skating over her body in twin spirals.

Yet she wouldn't back down. He might own her cooperation, might own her promise to fulfill her end of the bargain. But she was adamant that he did not own her. No man did. If she'd learned anything in the past few years, it was that her life was her own.

For better or worse.

"I don't think so, no. Because I don't believe for an instant you would withdraw medical treatment from Jacques, not after what you said to me earlier. Unless it was a lie? Unless you only said what you thought I wanted to hear?"

He gazed at her steadily, his face a mask of detachment. Her heart thundered. Had she guessed wrong? Would he withdraw his financial support? Would he let Jacques die?

Had she gambled too much?

Marcos looked so cold, so remote and cruel that she wondered how she'd ever managed to be infatuated with him all those years ago. Why hadn't she sensed that he was so brutal beneath that layer of charm he wore like a blanket?

Why didn't she just wear the damn necklace and keep her mouth shut? Jacques's care meant more than the principle of the thing.

"No," he said, dark eyes flashing with an emotion she didn't understand, "I would not stop his treatment."

She stared at him, her breath shortening at the admission. It was the last thing she'd expected. Marcos Navarre had a human side. A side that cared for more than having things his way.

Francesca bowed her head to hide the strength of her emotional reaction. He didn't need to know how much his statement moved her. But she would give him something in return, would make sure he understood that she intended to honor the agreement. Francesca d'Oro—*Navarre*—did not go back on her word once it was given. She had integrity, no matter what he believed about her.

"If it's important to you, I will wear the Corazón del Diablo."

Disbelief crossed his handsome face. "You just stated you would not. Most adamantly."

Francesca shrugged as if it were nothing, when in fact it was everything. "If you had asked instead of ordered…"

"Why does this Jacques mean so much to you, Francesca?"

She met his gaze evenly. "He cared about me when no one else did. Jacques is the truest friend I have."

"And Gilles? He is your lover?"

Her pulse throbbed in her temples. He didn't deserve an answer to that, not after the blood test he'd forced her to endure, and yet…

"No. And he never has been."

Marcos looked puzzled. "You are a beautiful woman. I wonder why this is not so."

Heat flooded her cheeks. "Don't say things you don't mean, Marcos. I think we know where we stand with each other now, don't you? You married me for the necklace, and I married you for Jacques. Please don't try and prop up what you assume is my wounded vanity. I know I'm not pretty enough for a man like you. And I don't care. I'm me, and that's enough."

He suddenly seemed amused, which only served to irritate her. It wasn't the first time this afternoon and she still didn't understand how he could find humor in any part of this situation. She looked away from him, out of the window at the passing traffic, and tried to concentrate on what it would feel like to be one of those happy tourists strolling along the sidewalk.

"You are quite different from who you once were," he said. "I like that you fight back. Livia would not get the best of you any longer."

Her chest felt like someone had turned a vise. She shoved the feeling away. "You would probably have married *her* back then if not for the necklace."

Marcos laughed. "You underestimate me, *querida*. Your sister has never held any attraction for me."

She whirled around to face him. "Everybody thinks Livia is beautiful. And you can't tell me you don't agree."

"No, she is quite beautiful—or she was eight years ago. And she knew it too." He picked up her hand, traced his finger along the edge of her wedding band while tingles of pleasure radiated up her arm. "But you have something far better than beauty, Francesca. You seem to know who you are. I like that."

A pang of hurt throbbed to life inside her. "It's taken me long enough," she answered.

His eyes were hot as they moved over her face. "I believe you always knew to a certain extent. But yes, something has sharpened your sense of self-awareness. I wish to know what."

She pulled her hand away, folded it against her body. "Shall we trade secrets like gossiping old ladies, Marcos? I'd not have guessed that was your style."

"I think you will tell me before our time is up," he said. He pronounced it with so much certainty that she wanted very much to prove him wrong, to knock him down a few rungs.

"You have far too much confidence in yourself. Not every woman feels the urge to succumb to your charm."

"But you will, *querida*."

"Not a chance," she vowed, though her pulse jumped at the look on his face. Where was that hint of anger he always viewed her with? When it was missing, he reminded her of the old Marcos. The Marcos she'd fallen for because he was nice to her.

He arched one dark eyebrow. His scar made the gesture that much more wicked. "You should not have said that, Francesca."

"Why not? Someone needs to tell you that you aren't irresistible. Besides, have you ever considered it might be your money and not your sparkling personality that makes women fall at your feet?"

Marcos laughed. The sound was rich, uninhibited. She liked it, much to her dismay.

"*Dios*, you are stubborn. But I never could resist a challenge." He leaned in, cupped her jaw in one broad hand, and kissed her before she realized what he was about. "I will enjoy taking you to bed, Francesca. And I will learn all your secrets while we are there, I promise you…"

CHAPTER SIX

THE SUN HAD dropped beneath the horizon over an hour ago. The air coming in through the windows had the bite of early spring, but Francesca did not move to shut the pane. She liked the coolness rushing over her skin. Funny to think that in New York it was fall and the temperature was probably the same.

The heat in her body hadn't diminished since the moment Marcos had kissed her in the car. She'd even stood beneath a cool shower as she'd prepared for tonight. The second she'd gotten out and dried off, the warmth came back.

How could her body refuse to cooperate with her head? Her head knew that Marcos was bad news. Her heart knew it too.

Her body, however, stubbornly wanted to straddle his and fulfill all the fantasies she'd ever had about him.

Francesca studied her reflection in the mirror. Her cheekbones were barely visible in the roundness of her face. She'd lost forty pounds in the last eight years, but still her face was too full. And her hair. God. Her hair was thick and unruly and hadn't been touched by a real stylist in years. Once, she'd had artful blonde highlights and lowlights incorporated into her tresses. Now, they spilled over into natural waves that weren't colored. The blonde wasn't as strong as it had once been, and she was afraid her hair was too brown. Mousy.

The last time she'd had it cut was a year ago. Now, it hung down her back, a long mass of naturally curly spirals that were anything but elegant.

She eyed the black dress hanging nearby with longing. And fear. They'd stopped at a boutique on the way home, Marcos insisting she needed a proper gown for tonight. All her efforts to choose something that flowed over her body without clinging anywhere were thwarted as Marcos instructed the shop girl to dress her in something strapless and form fitting.

When she'd emerged in this dress, her breasts shoved into a push-up bra and her waist corseted so tight she'd never be able to bend over, he'd looked mildly surprised. And interested, in a way she'd have never thought possible. For the first time, she'd begun to believe that maybe he wasn't lying when he said he intended to bed her.

And that scared the hell out of her.

Because Marcos Navarre was still the sexiest man she'd ever known. Even his scar was sexy. The more she was with him, the more she wanted to kiss her way across his jaw, to feel the silvery zigzag beneath her lips before claiming his mouth in a kiss.

Stop.

Thoughts like those were dangerous. She couldn't really be vulnerable to him anymore. It was a long time ago, and she was an entirely different person. She was no longer naïve or innocent, no longer believed the best of people.

With one last look in the mirror, Francesca gathered a shawl and the tiny studded purse that matched the dress, and made her way down to the foyer. Marcos was talking with the majordomo. When he turned to her, the words he'd been speaking seemed to die away.

His gaze raked over her. She stood stiffly, more uncomfortable than she cared to admit in clothes that clung to, instead of masking, her faults. Why hadn't she insisted on the kind of garment she preferred?

Marcos came over and took her hand. When he lifted it to his lips, the shiver that slid down her body wasn't entirely surprising.

The force of it was.

"You look lovely, *mi esposa*."

"So do you," she said, and then cursed herself for the inanity when he chuckled.

But he was lovely. The tuxedo he wore had been custom fit to his powerful body. The shirt was as white and crisp as new snow, the jacket and pants as black as sin. Marcos was tall and imposing. He smelled expensive, and he looked absolutely edible.

Just as he had the night she'd broken into his room and held him at gunpoint.

He hadn't forgotten it either, if his expression was any indication. "Perhaps we can play cops and robbers later, yes?" he rumbled in her ear, his lips brushing her cheek as he withdrew. "Though I hope you won't mind if we only pretend there is a gun."

"I might need a real one," she said. "It helps get me in the mood."

Marcos laughed. The sound surprised her. Sent an answering grin to her lips. God, he was sexy.

She wiped the smile away as quickly as she was able. She did not need to be too friendly with him. She didn't really believe she was in danger of being charmed the way she'd once been, but she could take no chances. It was safer to keep her emotional distance from this man.

"You look far too serious, Francesca," he said. "It's a cocktail reception for a charity I support, not a guillotine we are going to."

"I haven't been to an event like this in years. I don't know what to do anymore." There was no sense hiding it from him; he would know soon enough when she tried to fade into the background.

"It will come back to you," he said with more confidence than she felt. "You've spent the last several years running a shop—how could you not be a natural at interacting with people?"

"That's different."

"I doubt that," he replied. His gaze skimmed over her once more. "You need something else."

He retrieved a long velvet box from the antique foyer table. Francesca's stomach flipped. The Corazón del Diablo. She'd promised to wear it.

But when he opened the box, it wasn't the necklace she'd expected. The jewels sparkling against the deep blue velvet were cool and green. Emeralds of the finest variety. Her practiced eye skimmed over them: they would have cost him a fortune.

Though of course he hadn't bought them for her, she reminded herself. No doubt he'd had them locked away and pulled them out for tonight. But why hadn't he brought the Corazón del Diablo? She gazed up at him as he took the necklace from the box.

"Another time, perhaps," he said. "This is better for tonight."

Francesca hesitated, then turned and held up her hair

while he laid the stones against her collarbone. One egg-shaped emerald dripped into the shadow of her cleavage. The stones were cool in their platinum settings, but she welcomed the shivery feeling.

His fingers brushed the back of her neck, sending prickles of heat up her spine, down her back. She couldn't stop the ripple of a chill.

Marcos's hands settled on her shoulders, pulling her back against him. His lips touched her ear. "You look beautiful, *querida*."

Her silly heart thrummed at the compliment. Her head told her not to believe it.

"I believe this time," he continued, "our wedding night will end as it should."

Marcos watched his new bride as she stood nearby, engaging in polite conversation with a group of ladies. She looked as elegant and polished as any of them, and if she were at all nervous or uncomfortable, she hid it well. Not that he'd expected anything different. She was, after all, a d'Oro female. She'd grown into a woman every bit as elegant as her mother and sister had been.

His eyes skimmed down her lush form. She'd protested over the dress, but she looked fabulous in it. How could she look in the mirror and not know how very enticing she was? And why did she insist on wearing shapeless clothes that hid her curves?

He sipped the glass of wine a waiter handed to him and studied the sleek lines of one leg as the side slit in her dress opened. He had a sudden urge to go to her, but he'd been caught in conversation with an elderly matron. The woman nattered on about something he ignored—until she began to speak of teaching proper manners to orphans.

Nothing else could have so effectively ruined his mood.

"Señora," he cut in suddenly—sharply if the startled look on her face was any indication, "the street children of Buenos Aires need more than etiquette lessons to improve their situation in life." He gave her a clipped bow. "If you will excuse me."

He didn't look back to see how the woman was taking his abrupt exit. *Dios.* One of the things that drove him insane about these kinds of events were the wrong-headed ideas people who'd never suffered from hunger a day in their lives had about the children he so desperately wanted to rescue.

No child should suffer the way he knew that many of them did. Manners were laughable when survival was the goal.

The crowd of elegantly clothed people fell away as he approached his wife. She looked up as Marcos arrived by her side. Her eyes clouded when she saw him. Surprisingly, a sharp pain pierced a spot right below his heart when she looked at him like that.

Like he was evil incarnate, a devil come to steal her soul.

He shoved the pain down deep and held out his hand. "Come, Francesca," he said. "I wish to dance."

He didn't really, but it was as good an excuse as any to hold her. He did not ask himself why he wanted to do so. He simply knew that he did.

"I—" Whatever she was about to say, she changed her mind. "Yes, of course." With a polite word to her companions, she put her hand in his and let him lead her to the dance floor.

The music was soft, slow, flowing around them as he drew her into his arms. She gazed up at him, her smile gone. In its place was a frown.

"Why do you smile for everyone but me?" he asked.

She seemed startled, but she quickly masked it. "That's not true. And I could ask why you look so severe. Did I do something wrong? Have I mixed the fish fork with the dessert spoon again? Seated the priest beside the prostitute?"

She was trying hard to be irreverent, but the catch in her voice surprised him. He worked to force away the dark clouds wreathing his mind. "It's nothing."

"You say that quite a lot, Marcos," she said, her gaze on the center of his chest as they moved.

"Do I?"

"You do. Last night, and this morning when I asked you about the tattoo."

Her eyes were troubled. He looked away, over her head at the sea of dancers. She almost seemed worried about him. He didn't like the way that made him feel. Like he wanted to share things with her, to make her understand.

She intrigued him like no on else, and he wasn't accustomed to it.

"There are things I don't wish to talk about, with you or anyone."

"Sometimes it helps to talk about the things that trouble us."

"Really? Do you intend to share your secrets with me? To tell me why you refuse to believe a man could want you, or why you love this Jacques Fortier so much that you would risk your life for him?"

"I never said a man couldn't want me. I said I wasn't the usual type of woman you were attracted to."

"Ah yes, you know so much about me. I had forgotten. And what about Jacques, Francesca?"

She refused to look up at him as they swirled across the floor. "I told you he took care of me when no one else would. I—I was very ill. He nursed me back to health."

He didn't like the way the thought of her being sick pierced the shield around his heart. "You are well now? It is nothing that will return?"

"I'm recovered, Marcos," she said, meeting his gaze with an evenness that somehow seemed contrived. "No lingering effects."

"You wished to return the favor, yes?"

"Absolutely. Jacques saved me, and I want to save him."

"Then you will be pleased to know I've had an update from the hospital. They believe he is a good candidate for an experimental treatment with a high success rate."

Her eyes filled with tears and she blinked rapidly to keep them from falling. "Really? They think they can save him?"

"There is no guarantee, Francesca. He is very sick. But they have hope."

"Why didn't you tell me earlier?"

"I have only just had the call since we've been here, *querida*. They needed my authorization to begin."

"Your authorization? Gilles is his next of kin."

"Yes, but I am paying. And this particular treatment does not come cheaply."

She fixed her gaze on his chest again. The tip of her nose was red, he noted. She was struggling not to cry. A pang of some emotion he couldn't name stabbed into him. What would it be like to have someone love you so much that your well-being was their first priority?

When she looked up again, her eyes were still shiny. But the tears seemed to be under control for the moment. "Why did you approve it, Marcos?"

He found he couldn't give her an easy answer. Why *had* he approved an expensive, experimental treatment for a man he didn't know when the usual treatments might also work, and at a lesser cost?

"Because it was the right thing to do," he said simply. "And because you would want me to."

He'd spent years being unable to care for anyone but himself. Now that he had money, how could he say that one life was worth less than another? That he could only do so much?

He couldn't.

"You surprise me," she said softly, her tongue darting out to tease her full lower lip.

His body grew hard. In spite of everything, he wanted to possess her. Now, tonight. He was still angry with her, but he was also damned by this need for her. He needed to prove his mastery over her, to exorcise the demons of his past in the body of a woman. This woman. The reprieve wouldn't last, he knew, but at least he could have a few hours of blissful silence in the echoing chambers of his mind.

He stopped moving to the music and drew her closer. She trembled in his arms, her breath catching when she came into contact with his blatant need for her. Her eyes grew wide as she blinked up at him.

"*Sí*," he whispered, "I want you."

His head dipped toward hers, her mouth parting—in surprise or need he did not know. The moment their lips touched, the moment the electricity sparked and sizzled between them, a woman cleared her throat beside them.

"Señor Navarre, we are ready for your speech now."

Francesca's heart rate refused to return to normal, even after Marcos escorted her back to their table and held out her chair for her. A fine sheen of sweat rose between her breasts, on her limbs, heating her from the inside out. Her feelings were tangled and torn.

She watched her husband mount the podium and stand there, waiting a few moments for everyone to reach their seats before he launched into his speech. A single light shone down on him, making him seem completely alone in this crowded room.

He was so much more than she'd thought, and yet he was dangerous as well. That he'd actually approved an expensive treatment for Jacques stunned her. She knew he had the money—that wasn't it at all—but the obligation? He had no reason, no incentive, to do so.

He said he'd done it for her. Even now, that thought had the power to shorten her breath. *Why would he do such a thing?*

Because he was decent. Because he wasn't as cold and cruel as she'd accused him of being. Another feeling rose in her breast, a feeling she didn't want to acknowledge but had to nonetheless.

Shame.

She was ashamed that she'd stolen the Corazón del Diablo from him, that she'd held him at gunpoint and cuffed him to the bed. If she'd gone to see him, perhaps he would have helped her after all.

You have no way of knowing, Francesca. You did what you had to do.

Yes, she'd done what she'd had to, and the result was far better than she perhaps deserved.

If she weren't careful, if she didn't keep her emotional distance, she was in as much danger of falling for Marcos Navarre as she'd ever been. And that was something she could not afford to do. No matter how compassionate he might be toward Jacques, no matter how he claimed to want her in his bed, this was a temporary arrangement and the only heart at stake, if she allowed herself to feel as she once had, was hers.

Soon, Marcos lifted his head and the crowd quieted. When he began to speak, his voice rolled over the Spanish words with authority. She wished she could understand what he said, but she would have to content herself with the crowd's reaction.

"I will translate for you." A woman dipped gracefully into the open seat beside Francesca. "Marcos has told me you do not speak Spanish yet, so I will tell you what he says."

Francesca thanked her even as she tried not to imagine how Marcos knew this elegant woman. It did not matter. Francesca was a contract wife, not a real wife. She wasn't in love with him. Nor would she be.

"He is speaking of the orphans," the woman said. "Of our duty and responsibility to provide for the poor children of Buenos Aires. It is his passion, his life's work to create opportunity and stability for them, to lift them from the circumstances in which…"

Francesca's heart contracted as the woman talked.

Fresh tears sprang to her eyes at the horror of Marcos's words. He told of children who stole food to survive, who ate garbage and hunted rats, of children who learned to be hard and angry. Who joined gangs and became menaces to society.

She could see the passion in his expression, hear it in his words, and understand it thanks to the woman translating for her. When he finished speaking, the room erupted in applause. He looked alone, angry, and perhaps even a bit lost. Francesca glanced at the others, wondering if they saw it too. But no one seemed to see anything more than a very powerful, very rich man who asked for their support.

And she saw what she did not want to see: a man with heart and soul.

"He is quite a man, your husband." The woman held out her hand. "I am Vina Aguilar, an old friend of the Navarre family. I went to school with Marcos's mother."

Francesca blinked as she took Vina's hand. Though this woman was old enough to be Marcos's mother, she didn't look a day over forty. She was tall, lean, and dressed in a Prada silk gown that showed her trim figure to perfection. Her face was unlined, except for a few crinkles around the eyes when she smiled.

"You are not what I expected," Vina said after they'd chatted for a few moments. "But I am pleased for Marcos. He deserves all the love and happiness he has never had. I am sure you will give it to him."

"Yes, he does." Francesca dropped her gaze, hoping Vina would take it as shyness instead of the confusion currently pounding through her.

"Are you filling my wife's head with tall tales, Vina?"

Francesca's gaze snapped to Marcos as the woman laughed. He seemed perfectly normal again. Had she imagined the pain and anguish in his demeanor? The loneliness?

"Darling, I have said not a word that wasn't true," Vina replied, rising and kissing him on both cheeks. "And I was just about to tell your lovely new wife that I hope you will take the time to have a few children of your own. We need more men like you, Marcos."

"Gracias, señora," Marcos said while Francesca's head began to swim. He reached down and took her hand in his. If he noticed it was clammy, he did not react. "But we are taking time to get to know each other first. Perhaps later."

"Of course, of course." She suddenly waved at someone across the room. "Esteban needs me, darling. I'll write a check for the foundation, and I'll see you soon, yes? Bring your beautiful *esposa* to dinner."

Francesca couldn't look at him as he dropped into the chair Vina had vacated. Children? She'd wanted Marcos's children once. And tonight, hearing him speak so passionately about the lost children in the streets, she couldn't help but think that Vina was right. He did deserve children of his own.

Several people came by to speak with Marcos. Francesca sat there like a good wife, smiling and speaking with those who spoke to her, though her thoughts were far away. When Marcos eventually touched her shoulder, she jerked.

He frowned down at her. She hadn't even been aware he'd stood.

"If you are ready, we can leave," Marcos said.

"Yes, of course," she said, allowing him to help her up. "But shouldn't you stay to speak with the donors?"

He picked up her shawl and wrapped it around her. "The Foundation has a staff, *querida*. They are quite capable of handling the donations now that I've made the speech. And I've been speaking with people for the last half hour."

"How long have you been doing this, Marcos? I don't remember you ever speaking of this charity before."

He cupped her elbow and steered her toward the lobby. "The Reclaim Our Children Foundation is almost eight years old. I started it as soon as I regained Navarre Industries."

"How did you learn about these children?" she asked as they stopped under the portico to wait for their limousine. "I'm ashamed to say I had no idea this kind of thing went on in such a modern country."

He didn't speak at first and she wondered if he'd heard her. She looked up at him, surprised at the stark look on his face. He cared deeply for these children, she realized. And perhaps she was wrong to ask questions. Clearly, it was a painful subject for him.

"You don't have to—" she began.

"I learned about them firsthand, *querida*," he said, slicing her off in mid-sentence with his harsh words. "Because I was one of them."

CHAPTER SEVEN

WHY HAD HE told her what he'd never told anyone? His fiction had always been that he'd been sent to live with relatives. In the space of a moment, he'd told her the ugly truth.

Marcos poured a whiskey as soon as they were ensconced in the back seat of the limo and took a long drink. Francesca sat beside him, silent as the grave. She hadn't said anything since he'd spoken those ill-advised words. Not that she'd had any time. As soon as the words left his mouth, the car had arrived.

Now they were on their way, gliding down the drive and toward the street.

"I'm sorry," she said very softly. Marcos tilted the crystal tumbler back and drained it. Exactly what he did not want from anyone: pity.

"It was a long time ago," he bit out. "Forget it."

She let out an annoyed sigh. "That's your solution for everything, isn't it? Forget it."

"There is no point in dwelling on the past."

"But you can't forget it, obviously, or you wouldn't be so angry!"

He rounded on her, ready to lash her with words—except she'd finally let those tears fall. The ones she'd gulped back for Jacques Fortier were now sliding down her cheeks for him.

"Francesca," he said on a heavy sigh, "it's not important. The past is the past."

"But how did this happen, Marcos? What happened to your parents, and why didn't your uncle take care of you once they were gone?"

"Ah *Dios*," he breathed. What on earth had happened to his usual good sense in those few moments when he'd blurted out the truth? He didn't like talking about his past, yet he'd just told her one of the darkest secrets of his life. Not the darkest, certainly, but one of them.

He poured another drink and took a sip. Beside him, Francesca used the shawl to wipe away her tears. He handed her a cocktail napkin.

"My parents disappeared during the military *junta*. That was a time when people who were suspected of not supporting the government were quietly taken away and never seen again."

"You don't know what actually happened to them?"

He shook his head. He'd tried to find out, but the records from that time were not complete. The government had wanted no evidence of their crimes. "They were killed, Francesca, like so many thousands of others. And Magdalena and I were sent to an orphanage. When I was ten, I ran away. I lived on the streets for the next six years. Fortunately, she did not share my fate."

Her hand was cold where it grasped his. She squeezed hard, and though he did not want to accept her comfort, he found himself squeezing back.

"This is why you are so passionate about the children. It's very wonderful, what you do."

He shrugged. "Perhaps, but it can never be enough."

Though he'd set up the Reclaim Our Children Foundation, funded it when it was still in its infancy, made hundreds of speeches soliciting donations, and had the satisfaction of seeing children helped through the work his vision had created, it still affected him deeply each time he spoke as he had tonight.

He told himself he didn't care why wealthy people got involved, so long as they did. For some, it was the satisfaction of helping the less fortunate without actually doing anything themselves. For others, there was a true passion and desire to help the children have decent lives.

For him, it was the burning need to save every last child he could from his own experience on the streets. But he couldn't save them all, and that's why he felt so emotionally drained after these events.

"Marcos, my God," she said, straightening suddenly and leaning toward him with determination. "What you do is *important*. Never say it's not enough. You are making a difference in children's lives. Even if you can't help them all, saving just one from the fate you talked of earlier is extraordinary."

Marcos pressed the intercom button and spoke to the driver. Then he turned to Francesca. "I want to show you something."

She nodded, the emeralds at her throat winking in the streetlights. He reached out and touched the teardrop at the top of her cleavage. "I knew these would suit you. It's why I bought them, though perhaps you will think me quite shallow once you've seen what I am about to show you."

The pulse in her neck thrummed. He wanted to press his lips to it, but he did not.

Soon, the car slid into streets that weren't lit. Streets where garbage lined the sidewalks, graffiti covered the walls, and people scurried away like rats when the car crept through the alleys.

"This is where it happens, Francesca. Where they live."

Up ahead, another car was stopped and a youthful figured leaned against the window, talking to someone inside.

"That is either a drug deal, or someone looking for cheap sex," he said.

He could hear Francesca's breath catch. "Can't you put a stop to it?"

"No."

She turned to him, her eyes rimmed with tears again. "But you said—"

"This is what I meant," he replied, his voice harsher than he intended. "I cannot save them all. No matter how I try, there are those I cannot reach."

He tapped on the glass separating them from the driver, signaling the man it was time to go. The car accelerated and they were soon leaving the *barrio* behind and returning to the lit streets and vibrant life of the city.

"I know this shocks you," he said in the quiet stillness of the car.

"What shocks me," she replied in a hushed voice, "is that you are so much more amazing than I had ever realized."

Her words jolted him. In them, he glimpsed the eighteen year old with stars in her eyes. She'd wanted him for all the wrong reasons back then. He would not allow her to do so again. No matter how much he'd revealed to her, no matter that no other human being had ever learned as much about him as she, he would not lose sight of the fact that this was a temporary arrangement between them. There was nothing to build a future on. Nor did he want to.

Nothing was as she'd expected it to be. Francesca paced the confines of her room, her mind refusing to quiet and let her sleep. All her expectations and beliefs about Marcos had been turned upside down. Yes, she'd loved him blindly once, and only because he was handsome and paid attention to her when no one else did.

Those were not good reasons to love someone, of course.

Tonight, however, she'd been shown a side of Marcos Navarre that she'd never have guessed existed. After he'd left her eight years ago, taking the Corazón del Diablo with him, she'd believed he cared only for himself.

She'd blamed him for everything that had gone wrong in her life, yet in the space of a couple of days, she'd been forced to consider alternative views. First, that the Corazón del Diablo had always rightfully been his. That her father had killed himself not because of anything she'd done, but because he couldn't face what he had done.

And, most significantly, that Marcos had a heart beneath his hard exterior. He'd taken care of Jacques. He rescued children. And, dear God, he'd lived a life of hardship and deprivation on the streets of Buenos Aires.

She thought of the teen they'd seen leaning into the sleek car. Her mind couldn't help but wander toward another thought: had Marcos had to endure such things on the streets?

She'd told him he was amazing. Heat flamed through her at the memory. Had she learned nothing in the last eight years? Marcos might be more than she'd believed, but he didn't want her childish admiration any more than he ever had.

The way he'd ignored her the rest of the way home, and then excused himself once they'd arrived, was proof of that. It was their wedding night, and though she'd been afraid on so many levels of actually being intimate with him, she'd not expected he would go to bed alone. Especially not after she'd felt the proof of his arousal when he'd held her close on the dance floor tonight.

She did not kid herself about the strength of his reaction to her. He'd wanted her because she was available, because he'd married her and it was his right.

He'd slipped beneath her defenses tonight with his impassioned plea for those children, and with his shocking story of having been one of them. She didn't like the way it made her feel, the way she wanted to slip her arms around him and hold him tight. She should be relieved he'd gone to bed alone, and yet she was restless.

Francesca glanced at the bedside clock; the irony of the thought that this marriage had already lasted longer than their previous one came crashing through her. Yet she was as alone tonight as she had been that night so long ago.

With a growl of irritation, she yanked open the French doors fronting the veranda and stepped out into the cool night air. The thin cotton tank and sleep pants she wore were little protection from the chill, but her blood was so heated she didn't yet feel the cold.

"You wish to make yourself ill?"

Francesca spun toward the voice. Marcos emerged from the shadows, still clad in his tuxedo pants and white bespoke shirt. His tie was undone, and the shirt gaped open where he'd unbuttoned the first few studs.

"Not at all," she replied. "I couldn't sleep and wanted some fresh air."

"You should have put on a robe."

She wrapped her arms around her torso. "I'm not cold."

He moved closer. The shiny skin of his scar gleamed in the reflected light of the courtyard. He looked like a devil in the night. A very dark, very powerful, very sexy devil. Why oh why could he not be ugly and brutish? Why couldn't he be mean and cruel with no redeeming qualities whatsoever? Why couldn't she seem to keep her dislike of him wrapped tightly around her heart, like an impenetrable shield?

"You are shaking," he said softly, one finger reaching out to skim over her bare arm.

"It'll stop if you go away," she said. Let him figure that one out.

He tilted his head to one side. "You said that to me last night. But you aren't scared of me, Francesca. You might despise me, but you don't fear me."

She didn't know what to say to that. She wasn't even sure she despised him as much as she once had. Oh, she knew better than to believe she meant anything to him other than a means to an end—and that alone was reason enough to keep her heart locked up tight. But how could she despise him with the strength she'd had only yesterday?

She couldn't.

"What do you want from me, Marcos?"

"I want what men usually want, *querida*."

Her heart thrummed. "But why?"

"You really don't know, do you?" he said, his voice containing a kind of wonder.

"I know that I'm not the kind of woman you want. I've seen the photos of you from time to time. You date models, beauty queens, debutantes. I'm just a plain Jane, Marcos. I've always known it. I'm not polished or beautiful, and I'm not the kind of woman you would choose to marry of your own volition."

"You have always been lovely, Francesca. But I will admit that I have not always known it."

When he reached for her, she couldn't make herself move away, even though she knew she should do so. Her pulse was tripping and a sharp pain arced through her soul. *I have not always known it.*

She should put as much distance between herself and this devil as possible. Because he was bad for her heart, her soul. He was bad and dangerous and she trembled with excitement in spite of it.

Or perhaps because of it.

His body was big, solid. He caught her close and, instinctively, she brought her hands up to rest on his chest. Beneath the soft material of his shirt, his skin was hot. Her palms tingled.

Before she could speak, could think of a word to say in reply, his mouth claimed hers, hot and passionate—and perhaps even with an edge of desperation.

And she didn't care, because she felt something of that desperation too.

His hands slipped down her shoulders, over her waist, cupped her buttocks and brought her against the heat and hardness of his thighs. He was aroused, and her heart beat ratcheted up a level.

When his fingers slipped beneath her tank, she fought down a wave of panic. He would find her inadequate… he would change his mind and she would be humiliated again…

Slowly, he circled from her spine to her ribs and then up to cup the weight of one bare breast. A groan issued from his throat. The sound thrilled her. She'd forgotten what passion felt like, what those first moments of discovery in another's arms could be like. It was a drug—a heady, beautiful, natural drug.

His thumb whispered over the aching peak of one nipple. Francesca shuddered, but not from cold. Liquid heat blazed inside her.

He was the architect of her ruin, the instrument that had shattered all her girlish dreams, and her body didn't care.

She ached for want of him, for want of what she'd never had with him.

The kiss deepened, their mouths demanding more and more. Had she ever been kissed like this? Ever wanted a man as much as she wanted this one?

Francesca shoved the questions aside, torn between conflicting emotions. She hadn't been with a man in four years, hadn't wanted to be, and now she could think of nothing else but lying naked with Marcos, feeling the power of his body moving inside hers, watching the expression on his face as he found his release.

She wanted to wipe away the anguish and heartache she'd seen on his face earlier tonight. She wanted to be the one to make him forget, even if only for a little while.

Almost without conscious thought, she wrapped her arms around his neck, pulling herself closer, if that were possible.

She felt the heat and hardness of him, the rigid bulge of his arousal.

"I want you, Francesca," he said against her ear, tugging her shirt up to bare her breasts.

Too fast, too fast.

But she didn't want time to think, didn't want to realize she was making a mistake in letting herself be this close to him. Didn't want to know that to survive the experience, she needed to hide behind the wall around her heart.

When he stepped back to look at her, her arms dropped. She would have covered herself if he hadn't stopped her. Her shirt rested on the swells of her breasts, refusing to fall and hide her body from his greedy gaze. He lifted her arms out to the side, studying her.

"*Dios*, you are beautiful. How could you think any man would not find you so?"

"Marcos, you don't have to—"

He silenced her with a kiss, his hands threading into her hair. Then his mouth dropped down her neck, her collarbone. She knew what was coming, knew what he would do before he did it.

And she was powerless to stop him.

Powerless because she wanted it.

His lips fastened over one taut peak, teasing her, tormenting her.

Francesca gasped, her head falling back, heat spilling through her body as his tongue slid around and around her nipple. And then he sucked just hard enough to spike a shot of pure pleasure straight to her center.

The moan that escaped her was raw. Marcos made a sound of pleasure and repeated the motion.

And Francesca had to grasp his arms to keep from melting beneath his expert touch. Much more of that, and he could make her shatter simply from the pressure of his mouth on her breast.

It was exquisite, the pleasure. Surely she'd felt this kind of need before? Surely she had done so with Robert, with the man she'd nearly married before he'd walked out and left her to face the future alone?

Thoughts of Robert brought thoughts of her baby. Of the lifetime of loneliness she would lead because she could never have children of her own. Of the shattered fantasies she'd once harbored about having a family with Marcos Navarre.

Unbidden, a tear spilled down her cheek.

No, she would not cry.

But the tears didn't stop, sliding hotly down her face as he made such sweet love to her long-neglected flesh. She wanted more, and yet she cried.

Cried for her lost dreams and the barrenness that haunted her. She'd never believed that she had to have a child to be fulfilled as a woman, but having the choice taken away tormented her every single day.

A sob welled up in her throat. Desperate, she pushed him away and jerked her shirt down. Then she buried her face in her hands and let out the tears she'd been holding inside.

She thought Marcos would go, but instead he wrapped her in his arms and held her tight. The gesture was so surprising that she only cried harder.

"Come, you need to get back inside where it's warm."

"I'm f-f-fine," she said, trying to push him away again. Embarrassment was a sizzling wave of pain in her body. Why did she have to cry now? Why in front of him? How could she explain?

Marcos ushered her back into her room, then went into the bathroom and returned with a glass of water. "Drink this."

She took the glass, swiping furiously at her tears with the back of her hand. Marcos produced a box of tissues.

"I'm sorry," she said after a few moments.

"I would never force you into my bed," he said, his voice tight.

She blinked up at him. "That's what you think this is?"

He shrugged. He looked like a beautiful dark angel as he stared down at her. His snowy white shirt was open, revealing the v-neck undershirt that molded to his hard chest. She could see his pulse beat in his throat, see the tension in the set of his jaw and the vivid white relief of his scar. "What else?"

"It's complicated. But it's not you." Francesca gazed at the tissue in her hand, wadding it tighter and tighter. She thought of all he'd told her earlier, and suddenly she was too weary to hide her pain any longer. She wouldn't tell him all of it, of course. Some things were too private, too painful. "I was engaged. He left me and I haven't been with a man since."

She looked up, found Marcos watching her. The expression on his face said that he'd never considered she might have had a life after him. Perversely, that made her angry.

"I know it's a surprise, but yes, I actually had a fiancé that nobody bought for me."

"Francesca—"

"It's been four years, Marcos. And I find all of this here with you just a bit overwhelming."

He pinched the bridge of his nose sighing. "You must have loved him very much."

She bowed her head again and swallowed. She had thought she'd loved Robert for a time, but she'd quickly realized she'd confused companionship for love. "No. I was hurt, of course, but it wasn't the first time I'd had to deal with betrayal. I learned to be tough, thanks to you."

She should feel guilty saying that, since those events failed in comparison to the loss of her baby, but it was cathartic to accuse him of having had a hand in stripping away her naïveté. He had been a part of it, but not the biggest part.

"I'm sorry for your pain, Francesca, but life is not always fair. If it were, I'd have been raised in this house with two loving parents."

Shame flooded her. And the urge to tell him the truth. But then what? To do so would be engaging in a game of one-upmanship that was not fair to either of them. To try and top his pain with her own was wrong. It was not appropriate, not now.

"No, life is not fair," she agreed. "It simply is. And it could always be worse. Or that's what I tell myself anyway."

"Yes, it can always be worse." He seemed far away in that moment, his eyes unfocused and distant. But then he lasered in on her again. "Get some sleep. Tomorrow, we're flying to Mendoza."

* * *

She was awakened by a man yelling. Francesca bolted up in bed, her heart thundering. It had taken her a long time to fall asleep, especially after Marcos announced they were going to Mendoza where his fecund sister and her brood resided.

Now, she threw the covers back and headed across the hall. Marcos, whether he admitted it or not, suffered from nightmares. She could only imagine the things he dreamed about. Francesca tried the door handle. Amazingly, it ghosted open.

She hesitated for only a moment. Would Marcos be angry with her for invading his privacy? Probably, but she had to go to him. How could she let him suffer like this?

She crossed the threshold into the darkened room. Light from the courtyard shafted over the empty bed. Empty? Had she imagined she heard him crying out?

A groan sounded, and then a command in Spanish. It was definitely Marcos's voice, though grittier and harsher than she was accustomed to. She hurried toward the noise, then stopped short.

He lay in a tangle of blankets on the floor, his bare chest glistening with sweat. There was a scar across his abdomen. Shock rooted her feet to the spot. She'd never seen so much of his body before, had never thought he was anything but perfect. Had he been in an accident? She'd never asked him about the scar on his mouth. Perhaps he got them on the streets.

She shuddered to think about what he must have gone through.

He said something else in Spanish, his head twisting on the pillow. Francesca dropped to her knees beside him.

"Marcos," she said, touching his shoulder. "Marcos."

"No!" His hand flew up suddenly, as if he were about to strike her. Defensively, she grabbed his wrist. But he was strong, so strong, and the act of enclosing her fingers around his wrist only seemed to enrage him further. He shot up, his eyes snapping open, glaring wildly into the night.

Before she knew what was happening, he'd flipped her onto her back and stretched full-length on top of her. Both her arms were pinioned above her head, gripped in his strong hands that held her down so tightly.

"Marcos!" she cried. "For God's sake, it's me. Francesca!"

He seemed to hesitate. "Francesca?"

"Yes!"

"Dios," he swore. "I could have killed you."

But still he did not let her go.

"I was only trying to wake you. I didn't mean to startle you."

"You should not have come in here."

"I couldn't let you suffer."

His laughter was broken. "Ah, if only that were true, *querida.*"

Her heart went out to him. "What can I do to help, Marcos? I can stay with you. Or I can get you something. Just tell me."

His eyes were hot, but whether from the inferno of his dreams or the way he was now looking at her, she wasn't certain. She didn't understand what was going on, yet she felt it was changing so fast she couldn't keep up.

"What if the thing I need from you is more personal?" He flexed his hips then, the rigid form of his erection pressing into the cradle of her hips. Igniting an answering ache in her body.

"Then I would give it to you." She said it without hesitation, which both shocked her and aroused her.

His gaze slid down her body. Her nipples peaked beneath the thin cotton shirt as she thought of what he'd done earlier. His eyes lingered there for a moment. Then he murmured, "God, I do admit I am tempted."

His head dropped, his lips sliding along the column of her throat. The floor at her back was hard, but she didn't care. The hardness of his body pressing into her, the heated, shivery feeling of his lips on her flesh, and the anticipation of something far more explosive made the ache between her legs sharper. She wanted him, and right now she didn't care about the consequences.

She arched against him, enjoying the hiss of his breath as she did so.

"Then do it, Marcos," she said. "I want you to do it."

His mouth fastened over her nipple. She gasped, wanting the wet cotton barrier to be gone, but he made no move to lift her shirt away. No, he simply teased her nipple through the cotton, driving her insane with the heat and pressure that weren't quite enough.

"Please, Marcos," she gasped.

But instead of ripping her shirt out of the way, his head lifted, his eyes searching hers.

"Please what?"

"Please."

"You can't say it, can you? You want to tell me to make love to you, but we both know that's not what this is."

He let her wrists go and pushed himself to a sitting

position, his back against the side of the bed, his eyes closed. She propped herself on her elbows, confused and disappointed all at once.

"This isn't what you want, Francesca, not when you've been waiting for four years." He speared her with glittering eyes. "I'm not capable of tenderness at the moment. What you would get would be raw, hard and meaningless."

Her heart hammered. "Maybe that's what I want too."

Once more, he laughed that rusty, broken laugh. "I doubt that."

She sat up and wrapped her arms around her knees, the intensity of his words scaring her more than she would admit. "What do you dream about, Marcos, that torments you so much?"

"Demons, *querida*. Many, many demons." He stood and held out his hand. She took it and he pulled her up. "And now it is time for you to go. Thank you for waking me."

She pulled from his grasp before they reached the door, whirled to face him. "Why do you keep this locked inside? Why won't you let me help you?"

His face was a cold mask in the darkness. "You can't help me, Francesca. No one can."

"No, it's that you won't accept help. No one has to suffer the way you do."

"What would you know of it, *mi gatita*?" he demanded.

"I know a lot more than you give me credit for, Marcos."

He pushed her against the closed door suddenly, then stepped in and trapped her with his body. "My control is on a thread. You really need to go before I do something we both regret in the morning."

He kissed her hard, his lips demanding surrender. She opened to him without hesitation. He groaned low in his throat, gripping her ribcage as he held her hard against him and kissed her like he was a dying man and she his only hope of salvation.

She kissed him back without fear, her body igniting, her hope soaring that he would actually take her to bed and give them both the release they wanted.

They were moving and he was reaching for something—

And then he pushed her into the hallway and shut the door before she'd even realized he'd stopped kissing her.

CHAPTER EIGHT

THEY FLEW ON one of Navarre Industries' corporate jets to the Cuyo province. Bordered on the west by the majestic snow-capped Andes, the region was the center of Argentina's wine production and boasted acres of vineyards that were fed by clean, cool melt-water from the mountains. Though the area was high desert, the plain around Mendoza was green with cultivation.

Francesca slipped on her sunglasses as she followed Marcos down the stairs that had been pushed up against the plane. She felt as if she could go back to bed and stay there for twelve hours straight. She hadn't exactly slept well last night.

Marcos, however, looked as if he'd slept the whole night through. He was fresh, alert, and she wondered how on earth he did it. Because it had been 3:00 a.m. when she'd left his room. When she'd stumbled into the breakfast room at nine, he was already there.

They hadn't spoken much, except for polite inanities. It was as if the fiery confrontation of last night had never happened. More than once she'd thought to broach the subject, to crack open the fragile egg of their silence on the matter, but she'd been unable to do it.

What was there left to say?

A car was waiting nearby. She thought they would drive straight to Magdalena's place, had been trying to prepare herself for it all morning, but when they pulled into a shopping district, she figured he wanted to pick up presents for the family. She folded her arms over her lap and leaned her head back to catch a few minutes of sleep while she waited.

"Come, Francesca," Marcos said.

"Why?"

She couldn't see his eyes behind the mirrored sunglasses he wore, but she could feel them moving down her body.

"You need clothes. I neglected to take you shopping before we left Buenos Aires."

"I have enough for a few days," she said. "Surely this can wait."

He removed the glasses. "What you have is not suitable."

Heat burned into her cheeks. "Why not? Are we attending a masked ball or something?"

"What you have is not suitable for you, *querida*." He waved his hand up and down her body. "These shapeless garments are not flattering."

She sat up straighter. She was wearing her favorite summer dress, a loose garment that flowed to her ankles. She thought it was feminine and pretty. "My wardrobe didn't seem to be a problem last night."

"Because we bought you a gown."

"I wasn't talking about that."

"Ah," he said. "Clothes, in that instance, are irrelevant. But you are beautiful, Francesca, and you need to wear clothes that show your gorgeous body."

"I like this dress," she said militantly.

"It belongs to someone two sizes larger."

She stared at him for a long minute. She'd had this dress for a few years—and she'd worn it when she was twenty pounds heavier. That he knew it was for someone bigger surprised her. And embarrassed her. She grabbed the handle and ripped open the door.

"Fine," she said. "Let's go. But we're only getting a few things."

He inclined his head. "As you wish."

Francesca marched into the first store, her dignity sorely bruised. But the shopping wasn't as excruciating as she expected. Marcos stayed out of it, mostly, but the shop girls refused to let her take a wrong turn. When she chose a garment that was a little too big or loose, they steered her toward something else. By the time they got back into the car, more than two hours had passed.

She hadn't selected much, but it seemed as if the boxes and bags had somehow multiplied on their way out to the car. She hadn't wanted to accept any more from him than she already had—the jewels last night still stunned her, but she knew that even if he'd bought them with her in mind, he had not bought them for her—yet she'd had to acknowledge she might feel more confident meeting his sister if she were dressed a bit more elegantly.

In spite of the new cream linen dress she'd changed into at the last store, Francesca began to panic as the car moved through the sycamore-studded landscape. They were getting closer and closer to meeting Magdalena and her new baby. When they finally turned in at a sprawling Spanish-style villa south of town, Francesca had to remind herself not to wipe her sweaty palms on her new dress.

As the car rolled down the drive, she braced herself
for whatever would come next. She expected children to
scamper out of the huge carved wooden double doors,
a man and woman to linger with smiles on their faces
and a baby in their arms as they welcomed Marcos to
their home.

And her, of course. But what would his sister think
of her? Especially if she couldn't look at the woman for
fear of losing control of her rioting emotions?

She'd thought she'd put it behind her. The fear, the
loss, the reality of what had been taken from her. She
could not change the past, could not reclaim what had
been stolen. There was only the future.

Yet the prospect of spending time with a happy family
terrified her.

A happy family.

As the car came to a halt, Francesca watched the door
to the villa, gathering her strength and preparing for the
ordeal of meeting Marcos's family. No one emerged, and
Marcos exited the car. The chauffeur came around and
opened her door. She stepped out of the car, shading her
eyes against the setting sun. The air was warmer than in
Buenos Aires, and fragrant with the scent of an orchard
nearby.

Plums perhaps?

Finally, the doors opened and a small man dressed
in black pants and a white shirt hurried over to Marcos.
The two exchanged words in Spanish, and then the man
was grasping a suitcase and yelling instructions to the
youngsters who came running from the interior.

Their luggage disappeared as Francesca stood
there blinking at the scurrying children. Teenagers,
actually.

"They work here," Marcos said, as if sensing her confusion. "For me."

"But I thought this was your sister's home…"

"Magdalena and her family have their own winery."

"This is your home?" She tilted her head back, taking in the Spanish portico, the stucco and wood beams, and felt a relief she hadn't expected flood her senses.

"*Sí*. This is the *Bodega Navarre*. We grow olives, plums, and grapes here. The children help make the oil, wine, and jellies. They sell it to tourists and…"

Francesca ceased listening. A buzzing started in her ears and wouldn't stop. Marcos employed the kids that he wanted to save from the streets. He'd said he didn't do enough, yet he did more than he'd told her. He'd talked of hiring the kids, teaching them a trade, giving them something meaningful to do while they were schooled properly. She thought he meant through the Foundation, not that he personally did this.

In his home, with his money.

Oh God.

Her heart wasn't going to survive this experience. She already knew he was decent, that he cared for people and used his money for good. She'd thought she was safe to like him again.

But this. *This.*

She couldn't forget why she was here. Marcos Navarre simply wanted her for the Corazón del Diablo. It didn't matter if he was kind to orphans, or if he took care of needy children, or if he had nightmares that she didn't understand.

This was about the necklace, and his ownership of it, nothing else. He might realize that she wore clothes that didn't fit, but that didn't mean he cared for her. She'd been in Argentina for three days and she was already questioning her beliefs. How on earth would she survive for three months?

"Francesca."

She shook herself when he repeated her name. "Yes, sorry, just thinking."

He held out his arm. "Come inside. Ingrid will have prepared an amazing meal, and you must surely be hungry by now."

She was surprised to realize that her stomach was growling. "I am, yes."

Marcos showed her to a room, left her to freshen up, and said he would meet her in fifteen minutes outside her door. After a quick brush of her hair and a swipe of fresh lip-gloss, she emerged to find Marcos waiting for her. Her heart tumbled into her toes, then soared to the top of her head. He looked delicious, of course. He wore faded jeans and he'd loosely rolled the sleeves of his white cotton shirt. He'd also exchanged his polished loafers for a pair of flip-flops.

She thought he would take her to the dining room, but instead he showed her outside, to the covered veranda, where a table had been set up with linens, crystal, silver and china. Instead of a single rose, a spray of wild flowers bloomed in a vase in the center of the table.

Beyond the veranda, the cobbled terrace gave way to a manicured lawn that flowed naturally into the vineyard beyond. Vines twisted along the fences that lined each row. The back of the house faced west, so that beyond the vines she could see the snowy peaks of the Andes.

"It's beautiful," she said.

"*Sí.*" Marcos pulled her chair out for her. "I love to come here, when I can get away."

Once they were seated, a young man arrived with a bottle of wine. Marcos tested the small splash he was given, then nodded and said something in Spanish. The boy grinned and poured a full measure into Marcos's glass before coming to pour for her.

When he was gone again, Marcos lifted the glass and held it up to the light. "It is a Malbec," he said. "The grapes originally came from France, but they like Argentina better."

He sipped and closed his eyes. She watched the slide of his throat as he swallowed. Her mouth was suddenly dry as she sipped her own wine. She closed her eyes too, more to block out the sight of Marcos drinking than because she thought it would add to the experience.

The wine was fruity and full-bodied: plummy, with flavors of spice, currant, and vanilla.

"It's delicious," she said. "Do you make this here?"

He nodded. "We have a vintner on staff. The wine is mostly for Navarre Industries, though we sell some to the tourists."

"Why did you say you don't do enough for the kids? I can't imagine that anyone could do more."

He shrugged, but she knew the gesture was anything but light. "You have seen what I am up against. There are more kids every day who find themselves in the streets, begging, doing drugs, selling their bodies. Many have families to return to at the end of the day, families who live in shacks and who need the income they produce. Others have nowhere to go. The Foundation has better luck with them, but we try to reach them all."

"I think you're doing a wonderful job, Marcos..."

The words died in her throat as a black haired toddler came running out of the nearest door on chubby legs, a girl chasing him as he giggled and screamed. Marcos was on his feet in an instant, scooping the child into his arms before he could get away. The girl, a golden blonde creature who looked no more than twelve, stood with her head bowed and her hands behind her back.

"Señor Navarre," a tall, blonde woman who must be the girl's mother said as she hurried out of the house, "please forgive me. I turned my back for two seconds, and he was gone. Isabelle was trying to catch him for me."

Marcos smiled at the toddler who was clinging to him and giggling. "It's not a problem, Ingrid. And who is this little one?"

The woman wiped her hands on an apron as she came forward. "He belongs to Ana Luis, one of the new girls here. His name is Armando."

"Ah, I see." Armando's eyes grew wide as the food began to arrive. He bounced up and down in Marcos's arms. Marcos laughed. "Perhaps he is hungry, yes?"

"I was just about to feed him, as soon as I finished frosting the cakes."

"Go finish. He can stay with us for a while."

"He will disrupt your lovely dinner, señor."

Marcos smiled, so at ease for a moment that Francesca had trouble believing this was the same man who had violent nightmares. "We will cope."

Ingrid nodded. "I'll send Isabelle back with his food."

"Bueno."

The woman and girl left, and Marcos sat down with Armando on his lap. Francesca's heart had stopped beating minutes ago. Now, it lurched forward painfully as the boy gabbled nonsense and reached for the hot plate a waiter had set in front of Marcos.

"No, little one," Marcos said. "Be patient."

Francesca tried to concentrate on the food as it was being delivered. The scent of the steaks was divine. Besides steaks—*bife di lomo*, served with a *chimichurri* sauce—there were steaming vegetables, fragrant rice, and hot empanadas.

Someone brought an extra fork. Marcos put a little bit of rice on it and, once he tested it for heat, fed it to the boy. Isabelle returned with a plate of cut up steak and vegetables and set it near Marcos.

"You are a natural with children," Francesca managed as she cut into her own steak, her heart throbbing so painfully it was a wonder she could still speak. The little boy in Marcos's lap was adorable, with silky black curls, a bow mouth, and the smoothest olive skin she'd ever seen. When he looked up at her, long eyelashes framed dark eyes that watched her so solemnly.

What would her baby have looked like? Her little girl. She dropped the fork and pressed a hand to her mouth. She'd only just found out her baby was a girl a couple of weeks before the robbery.

Marcos was watching her, his brows drawing low. "What is wrong, Francesca? Something does not agree with you?"

She shook her head, swallowed. Forced her shaking hand to pick up the fork and knife again. "It's nothing."

"I seem to recall you taking me to task for saying this very thing. Are you quite sure?"

She forced a smile. "I'm quite sure it's nothing I wish

to talk about." She nodded at the little boy. "Armando is hungry."

"Do you wish to feed him?"

Francesca shook her head. Her food was a lump of sawdust in her stomach. "Let's not disrupt him when he's so happy with you."

Marcos fed the child another bite of steak. "Do children frighten you?"

"A bit," she said. "I don't know a thing about babies."

"I think you would be a good mother, Francesca."

Her pulse throbbed. "What makes you say that?"

"Because you have a kind heart. When you love someone, you love with your whole being. If you would go to such lengths for an old man you care about, what would you not do for your own child?"

Francesca put her napkin on the table. It was as if Marcos could see into her soul—and she didn't like the feeling one bit. She felt raw, exposed, as if he knew more about her than anyone ever had. Coming here had been a mistake. Except she hadn't had a choice, had she? To save Jacques, she'd made a deal with the devil. She just hadn't expected the payment to be so brutal.

"I'm afraid I didn't sleep so well last night," she said, standing. "I feel a headache coming on, so I think I'll go lie down."

Marcos looked concerned. "But you have not eaten. Surely that will help."

"I'm not very hungry after all."

Francesca didn't wait for a reply as she turned away. She simply couldn't look at the man and child any longer, at how natural they looked together. Marcos was meant to be a father, but she was not the woman who could give that to him.

And that knowledge hurt far more now than it would have only a few days ago.

Francesca couldn't sleep. She'd spent the evening in her room, watching the small television, flipping through magazines, and trying to read a book. She'd been starving after a few hours, but just when she was ready to leave her room in search of food, a girl arrived with a tray. Sent by Señor Navarre, she'd said. Francesca had thanked her and taken the tray to her bed, where she finished everything on the plate and tried not to think about the fact that Marcos had been considerate enough to send her food.

Now, Francesca climbed from bed and pushed back the curtains. The waxing moon was in the gibbous phase, not quite full yet, slanting down over the vineyard and illuminating the rows. She dragged on a pair of jeans, a light sweater, and her tennis shoes. It was late, but a walk in the brisk air would do her a world of good right now.

The night was quiet as she emerged from the darkened house. A light burned in one window. Someone else couldn't sleep, or maybe they were afraid of the dark. She wondered about Armando, about his mother Ana Luis. Perhaps the little boy couldn't sleep, and Ana was trying to soothe him. He was truly an adorable child. He had the dark curls that she imagined a child of Marcos's might have. A pang of regret shafted through her at the thought.

Francesca walked down the manicured lawn and crossed the edge of the vineyard. The rows were straight, narrow, but not as filled with vegetation as they would be once the season progressed. The leaves were new, the vines still growing from the hardened, twisted stumps in the ground. It always amazed her to see a grapevine, to see how the roots were so gnarled and looked almost dead. But every year, faithfully, vines shot forth onto the wired rows meant to hold them. Without fail, beauty grew from the twisted, ugly stumps.

She walked deeper into the vineyard, emerging at a spot where the rows crossed into another direction. A lone tree stood at the center of the clearing. Another gnarled beast, she decided, recognizing it for an olive tree. But why a single tree in the center of the vineyard?

Something moved at the mouth of the row across from her. Her heart shot into her throat and she turned as if to run back toward the house.

"Who's there?" a voice said.

Relief cascaded through her. And heat. Always, always the heat. "It's me," she said, "Francesca."

She could make out the white of his shirt, the darkness of his jeans as he moved toward her.

"What are you doing out here?"

"I couldn't sleep," she said. "You?"

He stopped in front of her. Scraped a hand through his hair. "The same."

He smelled good, like spice and citrus and outdoors. The warmth of his body reached out and enveloped her. Comforted her.

"Do you often walk at night?" she asked.

"Not in Buenos Aires. But here, yes. I like the quiet stillness of the vineyard."

Her thoughts exactly. "Why is this tree here? It seems rather lonely."

"I'm not sure," he replied, turning his head toward the olive tree. "It was always here. It is very old, I believe. We have a grove, but this tree stands alone."

"Maybe it's a special tree."

"Perhaps." He took a step closer. "And how is your head? Are you feeling better?"

"A bit, thank you," she said. "Did Armando finish his dinner?"

She could see the flash of his teeth in the moonlight. "*Sí*, he ate everything. And then he had a small slice of cake."

"You were very good with him."

He shrugged. "He is a child. It's not hard to please them really."

"I'm surprised you haven't married and had tons of kids by now," she said. "I'd have thought that would be one of your priorities."

"And what made you think that?"

"The Navarre Dynasty, the Corazón del Diablo. Who will you leave all this to?"

"There is Magdalena and her children. The Foundation."

She could hardly believe what she was hearing. "So you don't want children then?"

"I didn't say that." He took another step toward her. "What is all this about, Francesca?"

She shrugged, pushing her hands into her jeans pockets. "Just curious, that's all."

"I'm curious about something, too. I'm curious about why your engagement didn't work out."

"Robert decided marriage wasn't for him." She shrugged again. *"C'est la vie."*

"And you have not been with a man since. I find this extraordinary."

"It's not, really. I've been busy, and I haven't been interested enough in anyone to take the next step."

He hooked a finger in her jeans pocket, tugging her closer. "You seem interested in me."

"We're married," she said, her breath catching as desire shot through her limbs. "And it's part of your damn contract."

"So you would make love with me because of the contract?"

"I didn't think I had a choice."

A finger twirled in her hair. "You always have a choice, Francesca. But I think you will choose me."

"You are far too confident in yourself." But her blood was humming and her body was beginning to ache with need.

"No, but I am confident in this feeling between us. There is something…"

His head dipped, his lips ghosting over hers.

"Something?" she asked a touch breathlessly.

His arms went around her, pulling her in close as she automatically put her own around his neck. "There is something about you, something I very much want to explore…"

"But last night—"

"Last night was wrong. Tonight—tonight is right."

She didn't ask why it was right. Last night *had* been different. And, she realized, it wasn't worth traveling old territory when what mattered was here and now. She ached to soothe him, to take away his pain and his nightmares, but she didn't know how to do it.

All she knew was that she was ready for this.

Amazingly, unbelievably—she wanted him. Without fear or regret. There would be consequences, she knew that, but she was so ready to push past her fear and insecurity and experience this with him. With the man she'd once loved more than any other.

With the man she could love again.

Francesca shuddered as their lips met. What was she getting herself into? But, oh God, how could she resist?

His mouth was magical, his kiss insistent and confident. Her limbs softened, her body turning liquid. She was jelly in his arms.

He pulled back. "Unless you wish to make love *al fresco*, we need to return to the house."

"I don't care, Marcos," she murmured, pressing her lips to the warm skin of his neck. He smelled so good, so vibrant and alive.

"I might not either, except that we have no blankets—and the night is chilly."

She acknowledged that could be a problem. That and she didn't know what kind of bugs crawled around in vineyards at night. "Then I'll race you back," she said before sprinting into the night.

CHAPTER NINE

MARCOS LET HER win the run to the house. She hesitated when she reached the threshold, but he grabbed her hand and led her toward her room. The one thing he never did was spend the entire night with his lovers. Usually, he took them to hotels or met them at their place, but he rarely took them home to his. And when he did, he bundled them off before daybreak.

He did not sleep with anyone. Ever.

Francesca was the first woman to catch him in the midst of his nightmares, but still he would not share his sleep with her. He would make love to her—was dying to do so, really—but he would return to his own room when they'd exhausted each other too much for more lovemaking.

When they reached her room, she seemed to grow suddenly shy. She moved away quickly, before he could take her in his arms again, and busied herself with tidying up a stack of magazines on the bedside table.

"You are having second thoughts?" he asked, because he was never willing to dance around the truth.

"N-no, not at all," she said with a toss of her glorious hair. She looked defiant. Like a scared little kitten trying to be brave.

Marcos smiled. "Ah, *mi gatita*," he said softly. "There is nothing to be frightened of. I will be gentle with you."

"Who said I was afraid? Really, Marcos, you think too much of yourself."

He laughed. Then he unbuttoned his shirt and cast it off. The blood pounded in his veins, urging him to take her now, but he would not do so. He intended to use the utmost control, to take it slow and thorough. To make up for eight years of wanting. Surprisingly, the wanting was as much his as it was hers. He hadn't considered consummating their relationship back then, but since he'd seen her again, he regretted not having done so. An odd feeling, to be sure, but there was no use questioning it.

He crossed to her, while she watched with wide eyes, and wound his hands in her mane of hair.

"So much hair," he said, "so beautiful. I do not know why you never wore it this way before."

Her gaze dropped. He could see the pulse beat in her throat. And in that moment, he found her more attractive than he could ever remember finding any woman. Francesca had that killer combination of wide-eyed innocence and a deep sensuality she seemed unaware she possessed. He wondered, only for a moment, if this was another act, a metamorphosis of her persona eight years ago.

But, no, he didn't believe that. The woman who'd fought him for the sake of an old man she loved did not need to resort to playing games now. What would be the point anyway? They were here, in this room, and he was going to strip her slowly and make love to her for as long as he was able.

And, *Dios*, he was going to enjoy it.

* * *

Francesca felt like she was viewing the scene from somewhere up above. Surely Marcos Navarre was not standing before her shirtless and tugging her toward him by gently winding her hair around his fist. Surely his eyes weren't ablaze with heat for her? The bulge in his jeans was not because of her.

But there was no one else in the room.

She slipped her arms around his naked waist, the heat of his skin sizzling into her like a brand. Then she tilted her head up and closed the distance between their mouths before he could do it. She was afraid that if she didn't, she would wake and discover this had only been a dream.

The kiss was far gentler than she'd thought it would be, gentler than the kiss in the vineyard had been. It was as if he was trying too hard to be careful with her.

"Marcos," she said against his lips, "I'm not going to break. *Kiss me.*"

"I am kissing you," he murmured.

"*Really* kiss me. Like you mean it."

"Oh, I mean it."

She gasped as he cupped her face in both hands, his mouth coming down on hers hotly. If she thought they'd shared a passionate kiss before now, she was mistaken. *This* kiss was so much more, so full of heat and passion and longing that she didn't know how they'd ever make it to the bed before they went up in flames.

His hands left her face, slipped beneath her sweater and pushed it upward. They broke the kiss long enough for him to rip it over her head, and then they were kissing again. Francesca reached for the fastening of his jeans while he unsnapped her bra and tugged it off her arms.

She wrapped her arms around him again, and then she was pressed against him, naked chest to naked chest. The sensation was exquisite, so full of heat and sensation that she wanted to moan with the pleasure of it.

But then Marcos swept her into his arms, never breaking the kiss, and she clung to him with heady anticipation. A moment later, he laid her on the bed, following her down. It felt wicked to be here like this, him on top of her, both still clad in jeans, their bodies grinding together through the barrier of fabric.

She was on fire. Absolutely on fire. Arcs of electricity shot through her core, tingling into her limbs. Marcos broke the kiss and sat up as he started to remove her jeans.

"We need to turn off the light," she blurted.

He stopped what he was doing. "I want to see you. All of you."

"No—Marcos, I can't."

His brows drew down. "Why not? Because you think I will disapprove of something? *Dios*, you are a naïve woman."

She crossed her arms over her bare chest and bit her lip. "I'm self-conscious, that's all."

"I know this. And I intend to prove to you how beautiful you are to me." He stripped her jeans and panties in a smooth motion, then stood and shoved his own pants down his hips. His penis sprang free, glorious, erect—and, wow, more than she'd expected. "Do I look as if I'm turned off by your body, *mi gatita*?"

Francesca shook her head, a hot feeling bubbling up inside her at the sight of him. He was truly magnificent. And she was a very lucky woman right this moment.

Marcos stretched out over top of her, his weight pressing her into the bed. Dizzily, she thought it must be the most erotic thing she'd ever experienced—because she wanted him so badly, had wanted him for years. And she was about to have him. The anticipation was excruciating, amazing…

Marcos slid down her body. "I've been wanting to do this…"

He cupped her breasts, pushing them together so that he could suckle each one in turn. He used his tongue and teeth, licking and nipping her ever so lightly while she squirmed beneath him, the pleasure so exquisite she thought would surely expire of it before much longer.

"Marcos—oh…"

"You are delicious, Francesca. Everything a man could want…" he said against her damp skin.

His mouth made a hot path to her belly button, and then he was moving lower, pressing a kiss to her hip, her abdomen.

Francesca gasped as he moved lower. She would never survive it. Never.

"Marcos, don't—"

He said something in Spanish then, something hot and dark that melted the words in her throat, melted her fear. And then he was parting her thighs, gazing at her.

She wanted to pant with the anticipation of it. It'd been so long, so damn long since she'd felt pleasure.

Marcos parted her with his thumbs, and then his mouth was there, licking and sucking that part of her that had been neglected for so many years. Francesca didn't have even a moment to build up to her release; she shattered immediately, the world turning into a bright white burst of feeling that wrung a sharp cry from her before it let her go.

"Madre de Dios," Marcos breathed. "You are incredibly sexy, Francesca. Never doubt this."

And then he was taking her over the edge again with his lips and tongue, before moving up her body and kissing her while she wrapped her legs around his waist.

He groaned low in his throat, halting his forward motion. "I had intended to go slower, but I find I cannot wait. You must tell me if it's too much, if I hurt you."

"I'm not a virgin," she said, threading her hand through his hair and arching up until her breasts were touching his chest. How much she'd wanted to do this with him so many years ago, before she even understood what it really entailed. To let him be the first—and only—man in her life.

"You might be tender after so long."

"I really don't care. I want you, Marcos." How freeing to say those words, openly, and know he felt the same. At least in this.

She tugged his head down, fusing her mouth to his. Marcos must have surrendered to the inevitable, because he slid into her body in one long glide that took her breath away.

Francesca tilted her hips up, then gasped at the lightning bolt of sensation streaking through her. Marcos tore his mouth from hers.

"Don't move," he said harshly, his eyes glazing. "For God's sake, don't move."

She did it again, her breath snagging in her chest, her body sizzling. "But it feels amazing…"

So amazing she wanted to cry with the wonder of it.

His jaw was granite. "*Sí*, but this will be over far too soon if you don't stop moving."

She caressed his cheek, joy welling inside her, making her giddy. "Oh, Marcos, why didn't you tell me you had premature issues?"

He swore. And then he laughed, though she knew he tried not to. "Why do you amuse me even now? Is this not serious to you?"

"Very."

"And to me," he growled. Then he flexed his hips. A shiver began at the top of her head and rolled to her toes. It was so unlike anything she'd ever experienced before. All thought of teasing him flew from her head. Raw need was a clarion blast in her soul.

"Marcos—"

When he rolled his hips forward again, she couldn't remember what she'd been about to say. Couldn't think. Could only *feel*.

"Oh yes, *mi gatita*," he said, somehow still capable of thought and speech, "it is *very* serious indeed."

When he withdrew and surged forward again, Francesca was lost to everything but what their bodies did. The way they rose and fell together, their breaths mingling, tongues tangling, the rhythm of their thrusts becoming more and more frenzied. It was as if they fought each other, and yet it wasn't a fight at all. It was a tango, a beautiful dance that required each partner to give everything to the other in pursuit of satisfaction.

The air in the room was charged, zinging with electricity, and she felt as if she were drawing all of it into her body, concentrating it in her core until it would inevitably burst forth and incinerate her in the process.

It seemed to last forever and not long enough. She had no warning before she was flung into space, gasping and shuddering, her body dissolving into nothingness. She heard Marcos's groan of satisfaction, felt the power of his final thrust, the tremors in his body as he found his release.

A few moments later, he propped himself up on his forearms so as not to crush her beneath him. And yet she missed the pressure of his body, the hard hot feel of him melting into her. God, she'd do it again right this instant if she had the energy.

And so would he, perhaps, if the fact he was as hard as ever was anything to go by.

Francesca stretched, still floating on a cloud of satisfaction and unwilling to come down off it to deal with reality anytime soon. There was plenty of time for that later.

"And how did that feel, *mi gatita*? Was it worth the wait?"

"Oh yes," she purred. "Very worth it."

He laughed, then kissed the skin beneath her ear while she sighed. "And you said I was too sure of myself."

"You are. But Marcos?"

"Mmm?"

"Why do you call me *mi gatita*? What is that?"

His smile was genuine. "I call you my kitten because you are so fierce, and so sweet at the same time."

No matter how she cautioned herself against reading too much into it, her heart cracked wide open. She was allowing him to get too close, allowing herself to feel too much. She turned her head away on the pillow, stared at the tiny bug that swirled around the lamp. Would it get too close to the heat?

Was she in danger of burning up in Marcos's white-hot flame?

"You are thinking about something," he said. "But I want you to think only of me."

Marcos flexed his hips, and her body answered with heat and want that wasn't diminished in the least by the release she'd already had.

"Think only of me," he repeated. "Of us."

And then he made it impossible for her to think of anything else.

He was sitting in a darkened room, on the floor because there was no furniture, and he could hear the scritch-scritch of small rodents behind the walls. His wrists were bound in manacles. They'd stopped stinging hours ago. Now they throbbed. Throbbed because they were swelling from the raw wounds he'd opened by trying to pull free.

He couldn't see what they'd chained him to. Couldn't see anything. Could only hear the rats and smell his own sweat and blood. How long had he been here? He'd lost track of time in the darkness and deprivation of the last few days.

Nearby, something hissed, sending his battered senses into high alert. Marcos struggled against the bindings, uncaring that his wrists felt as though they were being ripped open anew.

The hissing grew louder, the dry coiling of scales on

the floor more precise as the serpent moved. Marcos yelled, as much to scare the snake as to express his fear—

"Marcos!"

He blinked. The room was dark, but he was in a bed. And he wasn't alone.

"Marcos, it's okay," a woman's soft voice said. "You're with me. There's no one here but us..."

Her arms went around him, her face tucking into the crook of his neck. His first instinct was to push her away.

But he didn't want to. He wanted to hold her, to let her drive the dreams away.

"Francesca," he rasped.

"Yes, I'm here." She pushed away suddenly. "I'll get you some water. You're so hot."

He grabbed her arm. "Stay. Please."

She seemed to hesitate, but then she lay back down and curled into him again. Her body against his was comforting, soothing. He stared at the ceiling. How had he fallen asleep here with her? And why didn't he want to leave?

He should push himself up, should return to his own room, but he couldn't seem to do so.

"Would it help to talk about it?" she asked very quietly.

"It's an old dream," he said, though that's not what he'd intended to say. "There's a dark room, rats, and a snake."

"Is this something that happened when you were a child? When you lived on the streets?"

He swallowed. How could he tell her it was worse than that? "Something like that, yes."

Her hand slipped over his abdomen, tracing the scar he'd gotten from a close brush with an enemy machete. "Where did this come from, Marcos? Does this have anything to do with your dreams?"

"No more words," he said, rolling on top of her soft body. "I can think of better things than talking."

CHAPTER TEN

FRANCESCA DIDN'T EVER want to leave the bed again, not when Marcos was in it with her. But hunger finally won out. She slipped from the bed and took a quick shower, her body still aching in places it had not in a very long time. But it was a very pleasurable ache.

She almost hoped Marcos would wake and join her in the shower, but then it would be even longer before she got any breakfast. Frowning, she thought back to the last time they'd made love, when he'd woken from his nightmare. He'd been so intense, so driven. She wanted to take away his pain, and the only way she'd been able to do that was by giving him her body.

Yet she'd wanted more. She'd wanted him to talk to her, really talk to her, and she'd wanted to feel as if she were important to him as more than a bed partner. He'd called her his kitten, and her heart still throbbed when she remembered the way he'd said it, but she had to remind herself it meant nothing in the scheme of things.

This was a temporary arrangement, and she was leaving as soon as it was over. She had to remember that.

But her heart didn't want to think about it. Her heart, dismayingly, only wanted to think of Marcos.

When she emerged from the shower, she dressed in one of the new outfits, a flattering cream silk tank and pale yellow Capri pants. It surprised her, but she had to admit that Marcos had been right about her clothes. These were far more suitable than the older jeans and blousy tops she'd been wearing.

She felt good, but whether it was the clothes or the afterglow from last night, she wasn't quite sure. Perhaps a bit of both.

She returned to the bedroom, a little kick of disappointment hitting her in the breastbone when she discovered that Marcos had gone.

Probably, he'd returned to his own room to shower and dress. What would happen now that they'd been intimate? Would he expect her to move into his room? Would he move in here? Or would they keep separate rooms and spend their nights like illicit lovers rather than a married couple?

So many questions, and none she could really answer. Voices issued from the kitchen as she approached. Curious, she peeked inside. Armando sat in a high chair, banging the tray, and Ingrid was gesturing wildly as she spoke to another woman. They turned when they saw her.

"Señora Navarre," Ingrid said. "*Buenas tardes.* If you would like to go outside, I will serve breakfast there in a few moments."

"Of course," Francesca said, though it still jolted her to hear herself referred to as *Señora Navarre.* "But what's wrong? Is it something I can help with?"

Ingrid sighed and glanced at the other woman. "Ana Luis has run away. She met a boy, and has left to be with him."

Francesca glanced at Armando. He seemed oblivious to his mother's absence as he shoved cereal around on his tray. "She left her baby?"

"Yes," Ingrid said with a sigh.

"Does Marcos know?"

"Señor Navarre has just been informed. He has sent men to look for her, I believe."

"When did she go?"

"Sometime in the night. I found Armando alone in his crib when I arrived. Poor baby," she said, reaching over to tousle his hair. Armando giggled. Francesca's heart squeezed hard at the sound. He had no idea he'd been abandoned. No idea he wasn't wanted.

Why could people who didn't care about children have them when she couldn't?

Stop. It was no use traveling that road. She'd been down it before, and there were no answers. Only heartache and pain.

Ingrid put a palm to her temple. "I have so much to do today, and no idea how it will all get done when I must watch this little one here."

"Why don't I take him?" Francesca said, shocking both herself and Ingrid if the look on the other woman's face was any indication.

"Oh no, señora, I cannot ask you to do that. This is your honeymoon! You must have fun, spend time with your husband. A baby would be a distraction."

"Nonsense," Francesca said. Marcos had told people it was their honeymoon? Her heart leapt just a little at that, before she reminded herself it meant nothing. "It's not Armando's fault, and I'm not doing anything anyway."

"You're certain?"

Hell no, she wasn't certain, if the reckless pounding of her pulse was any indication. "Of course."

Ingrid grabbed a rag and wiped Armando's face, then lifted him from the chair and carried him over to her. For a moment, Francesca wondered if she'd made a mistake, if she knew what she was doing, but Armando smiled and spread his chubby little arms wide. She took him, tears springing to her eyes as he wrapped his arms around her neck.

He smelled like a baby. And like cereal and sunshine. She wanted to squeeze him close and kiss his little cheeks. Instead, she took him to the veranda and bounced him on her lap while she waited for breakfast to arrive.

Someone brought a play pen and popped it open. Francesca thanked the girl, though she was pretty certain by the frown on Armando's face that he didn't want to spend any time in it.

"It's okay, Armando," Francesca soothed. "You can sit right here with me if you're a good boy."

The baby burbled happily. Francesca gazed at him in wonder, her heart expanding so wide it hurt. Her own little girl would have been almost four. She'd stayed away from children because it hurt too much, but holding this little boy right now felt like the best thing she'd done in a long time. Besides making love with Marcos, of course.

As if thinking of him summoned him, he suddenly appeared in the doorway. The expression on his face, she noted, was thunderous. It cleared a little when he saw her, and he even managed a smile when Armando turned to look at him.

"Have you found her?" Francesca asked as he came over and pulled out a chair.

"No."

Armando reached for Marcos. Oddly, she felt a little reluctant to let him go, but Marcos took him and tickled his belly. The baby laughed uproariously while Marcos made faces.

A pang of longing pierced her soul. She wanted this life. Wanted Marcos and a baby. Wanted nights like the last night, and days that were perfect and stretched endlessly before her like a sea of happiness. She wanted what was, essentially, a beautiful illusion. And she wanted it to be real.

"What will happen if you can't find her?"

"Ah, *Dios*, I wish I knew."

"What about Armando?"

Marcos looked at the little boy in his arms. "He will be taken care of."

"By whom?"

"I don't know yet."

It pierced her to think of this baby without his mother, but what could she say? She and Marcos weren't in a real relationship, and thoughts of the two of them taking care of Armando if Ana didn't come back were a pipe dream. "I'm sorry, Marcos. I know it hurts you to have her leave like this."

His expression was controlled. "I told you I cannot save them all. And Ana has run away with a boy she met. She has not returned to the streets. Perhaps they will even marry."

"What usually happens with the teens you employ here?" she asked, wishing to distract him just a little bit. To get him to focus on the positive results of what he did.

"Some of them go to university," he said. "Others choose a trade."

"Do many of them choose college?"

"Many do, yes. Navarre Industries hires them once they graduate, should they desire to work for us."

What he did was amazing, and yet he beat himself up so badly over the ones he lost. She didn't understand it. "And what would happen to them if you did not do this, Marcos?"

He looked solemn. "Drugs, prostitution, gangs, death. Even war," he added, almost as an afterthought.

One word stood out. "War?"

"*Sí.* There is much unrest in parts of Latin America. Guerilla warfare against what one perceives to be society's oppressors can be an attractive option for some."

Her heart began to pound. "I had no idea." She thought of the scar on his abdomen, of the way he dreamed so violently. Could he have gotten scarred like that on the streets? Or was it a product of warfare? Suddenly, she had to know the truth. "Is that what happened to you?"

His eyes seemed so hard, so cold, as if his emotions had frozen solid. "Do you really wish to know? Do you think you can save me if only you know what drives me? That the love of a good woman will keep me from reliving the nightmare?"

He was so defensive that she knew she must be right. And it saddened her. Made her ache for the boy he'd been, the young man who'd suffered so much. He hid it away inside, and it was killing him.

But he couldn't see it.

"Yes, Marcos, I do want to know. But I imagine no one can save you except yourself."

The food arrived before he could reply. Marcos let Ingrid's daughter take the baby and put him in the play pen. His little eyes had begun to droop, and soon he was curled up asleep with his thumb in his mouth.

The moment was gone, so she didn't expect Marcus would answer her now. He surprised her when he did. He looked pensive, a bit lost, as if it wasn't quite his choice to speak but as though he couldn't stop himself.

"I am not accustomed to talking about this with anyone," Marcos said once Ingrid and Isabelle had gone. "But yes, I was a guerilla fighter, Francesca. I saw battle, I saw despair and evil and the worst a man can do to another man."

"I'm sure you did what you had to do," she said softly, trying not to let the tears mounding behind her eyes fall. He would not appreciate any show of pity.

He sighed and leaned back in his chair, his food untouched. "I have always done what I thought I had to do to survive. I can't apologize for any of it, but I wish it had been different."

"I think I understand why you hated your uncle so much now. And why the Corazón del Diablo is so important to you." She leaned forward suddenly, grabbed his wrist where it lay on the table. His reaction was immediate. He jerked his arm away so quickly she found herself grasping air and wondering what she'd done wrong.

"Don't ever do that," he ground out.

She sat back and folded her hands in her lap. She thought back to how he'd reacted so violently in Buenos

Aires when she'd gone to wake him and grabbed his wrist before he could accidentally hit her in his sleep. What was it about his wrists? She wanted to ask him, but she did not. She'd already intruded enough on his memories.

"I was just going to say that I think you are too hard on yourself, that you push yourself too much and don't take the time to realize all the good you've done. You take the failures much harder than you celebrate the successes."

Marcos shoved a hand through his hair, swearing softly. She opened his wounds wide and didn't even know it. And she cut so close to the truth that it threatened to crumble all his defensive walls. He was accustomed to success, maybe so much so that he took it for granted.

"You are right," he said carefully. "I do take the failures personally. Especially the kids. But when I fail them, I lose more than money or prestige. I lose entire lives."

"But you also save lives."

He picked up his cup of *café con leche* and took a drink. *Dios*, he needed the caffeine. So much was changing, and so rapidly. He'd brought Francesca to Argentina to punish her for taking the Corazón del Diablo, and to cement his possession of it. He'd not brought her here to let her worm her way beneath his defenses. She saw through him, saw to the heart of him in a way no one else seemed to do.

Why was that? Because she paid attention? Because she was more perceptive than others? Or because she'd known him in the past and had years to consider his personality?

He did not know, but he didn't like it. Didn't like the way his perception of her was forced to undergo a shift from old beliefs to newer ones.

Yet he knew that if his choices were to put her on a plane this afternoon, or to have her in his bed later tonight, having her in his bed would win the battle. One night with her, and he was addicted to the rush he felt when he made love to her.

The feeling was temporary, he knew that from experience, but it was damned inconvenient as well. Still, he intended to make the most of it while this arrangement lasted.

Even if she did get under his skin with her too-sharp perception and pointed questions.

"Yes, the Foundation saves lives. I am happy with this, but I will be happier when we are no longer needed. I'm not sure we will ever see that day."

"No, perhaps not," she said. "But you will never cease working to make it so. Of that I'm certain."

He nodded, then glanced over at the sleeping child. "I will be happy if we can find and bring back Ana Luis. Her baby will miss her."

Francesca's eyes were shiny with unshed tears. "I don't understand how she can be happy without him. Perhaps she will miss him so much she'll come back on her own."

Marcos studied her. She looked…wistful. As if she longed for a child, no matter that she'd claimed to be afraid of them only yesterday. She'd looked happy enough when he'd found her holding Armando.

"You could be right," he said, "but I doubt it. She is a sixteen-year-old girl. A baby is probably a burden. She wants to be free, to have fun, and this little one is like a millstone around her neck, I imagine. She may love him, but she has probably convinced herself he is better off without her."

She blinked, as if she'd never considered such a possibility. "Or maybe her head was turned by this boy she met. Maybe she'll come to her senses."

"Is that what you did, *querida*?" he asked very softly.

"What do you mean?"

"With me. Did it take you very long to come to your senses? Or would you have followed where you thought your heart wanted to go? If I had taken you with me that night, eight years ago, would you have come?"

She looked away, toying with the half-eaten croissant on her plate. "I imagine I would have followed you to the ends of the earth, Marcos. Though I'm sure I'd have figured out the truth soon enough."

"The truth?"

"That you were only using me."

"As you were using me."

"You can continue to believe that if it makes you feel better," she said. Then she speared him with a glare. "But the truth is, if I had thought that asking my father to *buy* you for me would have worked, I probably would have done it. Because yes, I was that hopelessly in love. That deluded."

Her words pricked him more than he liked. *Deluded.* "How do you know that you did not ask him? You didn't have to say those exact words, after all."

"I never spoke with my father about you. I never spoke with any of them, because I was afraid of what they would say."

"And what did you think that would be?"

She thrust her chin up, a gesture he was beginning to recognize as a defense mechanism. It was her mantle of self-assurance settling into place, however tattered a mantle it may be.

"That I was delusional, that I wasn't pretty enough or smart enough, that you would never look at me twice. The list can get quite long if you want to hear it all."

Anger surged through him at the thought of her family saying such things to her. And they would have, he knew. At least her mother and sister would have. Her father had adored her, which was perhaps why her mother and sister had been so jealous.

"They would have been wrong, Francesca."

She snorted. "Of course. And you proved how wrong they were by leaving as soon as the ink was dry on the marriage license."

He leaned forward and caught her face between his hands, kissing her until she began to soften, until he could feel the blood rushing to his groin and feel the pounding of desire in his veins. "They could say none of those things now, and you know it," he said, leaning his forehead against hers. "Stop picking at old wounds. Life is about forward motion, not regrets."

She gently disentangled herself from his grasp. Her golden-green eyes were full of sadness as she searched his face. He felt like he'd been shoved beneath a micro-scope—and the scrutiny was becoming uncomfortable because it went so far beneath the surface.

"Then why don't you take your own advice, Marcos? Because from where I'm sitting, you're a man living so deeply in the past you can't even enjoy the present."

They had not found Ana and her boyfriend by night-fall. Francesca took turns with Ingrid and another of the women who worked there in playing with Armando. He was a sweet little boy, but he was beginning to get fussy the longer he went without his mother.

Surely, Ana must have done a few things right, or her son would not have bonded with her so strongly as to notice she'd been gone for a very long time. Francesca had just given the child back to Ingrid and decided to go for a walk in the vineyard when Marcos emerged from his office.

She'd not spoken with him since breakfast. Once they'd finished eating, he'd said he had business to attend to and shut himself away. He'd even had his lunch delivered and had eaten behind closed doors.

She'd thought he meant to ignore her completely after what she'd said to him this morning. Looking at him now, her heart contracted. "Have they found her?" she asked, hoping beyond hope that he'd found out something.

He shook his head. He looked so forlorn in that moment, so defeated. She wanted to go to him, wrap her arms around him. Tell him how she felt.

And just like that, the truth of what she was feeling slammed into her, stole her breath away. She loved him.

She loved Marcos Navarre. This time it was real, not the childish love of an infatuated teenager. He was far from the selfish, cruel bastard she'd thought him to be. He felt things deeply, and he acted with more dignity and morality than anyone she'd ever known.

Including her own family. Her mother was selfish beyond belief, her sister had always been concerned with herself and the way she looked, and her father indulged them all with bigger and better gifts and trips.

Not one of them had ever expressed concern over those less fortunate than they were. She didn't ever remember any talk about favorite charities or reasons other than tax deductions to give money away.

And she'd been just as bad, living in her shell and worrying about herself and her secret—or not so secret—crush on Marcos.

Yet, in spite of loss and pain and a difficult childhood, Marcos had dedicated himself to helping others.

And she loved him for it.

The thought sent a little shiver of heat and joy racing up her spine all at once. And fear.

Because he did not love her in return, nor was he likely to do so. This was a temporary marriage, based on his desire to reclaim his family birthright once and for all. At the end of their time together, he would stick her on a plane and say goodbye forever.

"How is Armando?" he asked her.

"He seems fine," she said. "Ingrid has taken him."

Marcos shoved a hand through his hair. "This has never happened before. I cannot allow that child to go to an orphanage," he finished fiercely.

Francesca finally conquered her paralysis. She went to him, slipped her arms around his waist and pressed in close, her head on his chest. He did not push her away. Instead, he squeezed her to him.

"Of course you can't," she said. "It won't come down to that."

"What a tiger you are," he murmured. "So fierce, so strong in your beliefs. I am thankful you've never been disillusioned."

She pushed back, tilted her head up to look at him.

"I've been disillusioned plenty, Marcos. But that doesn't mean I give up."

He threaded his fingers through her hair. "I do not give up either. Perhaps we are more alike than I thought."

Heat wound its way through her limbs, sizzling into her nerve endings. All he had to do was touch her—no, all he had to do was *look* at her—and she was on fire. She dropped her chin, certain he would see her heart in her eyes if she kept looking at him.

A baby's wail ricocheted through the house. Marcos stiffened, though she knew it wasn't out of annoyance or anger.

"We should go see what's happening," she said. "Maybe Armando will respond to one of us."

"*Sí,*" Marcos replied, taking her hand and leading her toward the kitchen.

The scene they entered into was one of controlled chaos. Ingrid was extracting her hands from a pile of dough, her skin too covered in flour and gluten to quickly be free, and Isabelle was cleaning up an oozing pile of spaghetti that had spattered on the floor, the table, her, and Armando. A stoneware bowl also lay on the floor, shattered.

Baby Armando wailed at the top of his lungs in his high chair. Francesca hurried over to help Isabelle while Marcos grabbed a wet rag and wiped off Armando's face. Then he lifted the toddler out of the chair, uncaring of the tomato sauce that got on his shirt as he held Armando close and began to bounce him up and down.

Armando kept wailing.

"Give him to me," Francesca said when she'd helped Isabelle pick up the broken stoneware. Marcos handed him over, and though he continued to cry, he began calming down as she crooned a song to him. A song she'd sung to her unborn baby at night when her little girl would kick and keep her awake. It had often worked, or so she'd convinced herself.

It worked on Armando too. He lay his head on her shoulder and stuck his thumb in his mouth, though he still sniffled and hiccoughed.

"He likes you," Marcos said, shooting her a smile that melted her insides.

"Only this time. Later, it could be you he prefers."

Marcos's smiled didn't waver. "I doubt that, *mi gatita*. He knows he has found a soft heart in you."

She turned from her husband, certain her face was red. Ingrid gave her a smile and a wink. Francesca couldn't help but smile back. She carried Armando into the cavernous living area and sat down on one of the long couches there. Marcos was close behind, his hands in his jeans pockets, his shirt streaked with red sauce.

He'd never looked sexier to her. She could imagine him being so tender and good with his own child, and her heart ached. She loved him, and she could never give him that.

A pain throbbed in her breastbone. He didn't want that kind of life with her anyway. This was not a true marriage, and she was not a true wife. She'd been so incredibly stupid in not keeping an emotional distance from this man.

But how could she have done so? Each new thing she learned about him was like a nail in the coffin of her determination not to like him.

She'd failed, and she would pay the price when the time came.

Marcos perched on the thick wooden coffee table in front of the couch. "And you said you were scared of children."

"I'd never been around them, is all," she replied, stroking Armando's soft curls. Her eyes filled with tears. She tried to hold them back, but one spilled down her cheek regardless.

Marcos leaned forward, his brows drawing together as he caught a teardrop on his finger. "What is this, *querida*? You have told me to have faith. Do you not take your own advice?"

"It's not that," she whispered, suddenly overwhelmed with all she wanted to say. With all she wanted to share. "I-I was pregnant once."

Shock rocked him back. "Pregnant?"

She nodded, unable to look at him, her heart throbbing. "I lost the baby at six months. There was a robbery at the store, and I was beaten. They killed my baby."

"Francesca, my God—"

"She was a girl. Jacques cared for me when all I wanted to do was die as well. It wasn't just physical, either. He saved me from myself."

"Your mother? Your sister?"

She shook her head. "He called them, but they'd disowned me. Because of the Corazón del Diablo."

"Madre de Dios," he breathed, visibly shaken. "When did this happen? What did they do to the men who did this?"

"It was four years ago, soon after Robert and I split. The men were caught. One of them died in prison, but the other two are still there. There's one more thing." She drew in a deep breath. "I can never have children of my own. The doctors say the damage was too great."

CHAPTER ELEVEN

HE DIDN'T KNOW·what to say. Shock, outrage—even despair—were the emotions crashing through him at the moment. He stared at his wife in disbelief. Francesca's head was bowed, her attention focused on the toddler sleeping so peacefully in her arms. She stroked his hair with a shaky hand.

She could never have children—no wonder she'd been so uncomfortable when Armando had first appeared. She'd told him she had a headache, that she needed to lie down. But what she'd needed, he realized now, was escape.

He wanted to destroy the men who had done this to her. Wanted to destroy the man who'd left her to face the future alone while she was pregnant with his child.

He shot to his feet, overwhelmed with hot emotion, ready to do battle for her and slay the demons of her past. Yet it was too late, as he well knew.

She gazed up at him. Tears slid freely down her cheeks now and she swiped them away with the backs of her fingers while she tried not to awaken Armando.

He was so gripped with feeling, with emotion he didn't understand. He needed to escape, at least for a few moments. He needed time to regain his perspective.

"It's okay," she said. "I understand."

He couldn't move. He wanted to go, but he couldn't. "Understand what?"

"You're angry, probably even horrified. And you're glad we have a contract, because we both know this is ending in three months. You aren't saddled with a barren wife for real."

As long as she lived, she would never forget the way he was looking at her right now. His expression was hard, angry. The scar on his face was white, and she didn't think he realized that his hands were clenched into fists at his side.

Perhaps she should have waited to see what he would have said, but the truth was she couldn't bear it. So she'd said it for him, because she was certain he would not. He would have told her how sorry he was, how sad, and then she would have been forced to murmur her thanks, all while holding this precious baby, who almost looked like he could belong to Marcos, in her arms.

She couldn't bear it, so she'd given him his out.

"Francesca, that's not at all what I was thinking."

She sniffed, and was furious with herself for doing so. Being weak was not how she'd survived those dark days, or how she'd gotten where she was now.

"It's all right, Marcos. You don't have to explain."

He sank down again, elbows on his knees, his hands steepled together. "I am angry, you are correct about this. Angry enough that I want to find these men and punish them for what they did to you. And I want to find this Robert too. I want them to bleed, Francesca. For you."

She sucked in a sharp breath. "That's not what I want," she managed, her heart zipping recklessly.

"I know this," he replied. "It's what I want."

She could see the warrior in him then. A man who said he'd seen the worst that one person could do to the other. He'd not only seen it, he knew how to do it. And she knew he was capable of it. A shiver washed down her spine at the thought.

"I will not do this," he continued. "But it's what I want to do."

"It's in the past, Marcos. Nothing will bring my little girl back now. If it would, I'd do it myself, believe me."

He was looking at her in a new way, she realized. Was it respect? Or pity? She couldn't tell, and she was too emotionally exhausted to figure it out.

"It is no wonder I didn't recognize you that night," he said. "You have changed, Francesca, and not only in a physical way. Don't you see how strong you are? How fierce and protective? How could you think that you are not unbelievably beautiful? You blind me with your beauty."

Armando stirred in her arms then, saving her from having to say something in return. Because, quite frankly, he'd stunned her. And given her hope. Was it possible he felt something more for her too? Was it silly to believe that maybe there could be something wonderful between them?

Marcos's cell phone rang. He answered it with a clipped, *"Sí."* And then, much quicker than she'd expected, he was finished. His eyes were dark with emotion. He reached out to stroke Armando's curls and shook his head, his jaw clenched tight.

"Marcos, what is it?" she asked. Deep inside, she knew it wasn't good. She could see it in his face, feel it in the air. Poor, poor Armando.

"They've found Ana."

"But that's good, right?" Hope beyond hope. *Please let this baby get his mother back...*

"She's not coming back, Francesca. Not ever. She and her boyfriend were drinking. There was an auto accident. They did not survive."

The house was in an uproar for several hours. Marcos went with one of the men to claim the body for burial. The teens seemed to come out of the woodwork now, their ability to concentrate on their tasks severely compromised. Ingrid rocked Isabelle, who cried endlessly. Though Ana hadn't lived at the winery for long, Isabelle had grown close to her in that short time.

Ana, it seemed, had been vibrant and fun, quick to laugh, a peacemaker and sweet girl who just wanted to be loved. It was that need to be loved that had led her to run away with a boy she'd thought adored her. No one knew who Armando's father had been, but they knew Ana had been in love with him once. He'd abandoned her and she'd ended up here, lonely and scared and still looking for love.

Armando was, thankfully, asleep in his crib. He'd begun to cry again when so many others were doing so, but Francesca got him to go back to sleep and he was currently bedded down in the room he'd shared with his mother.

By the time Marcos returned, it was late. Everyone had trickled back to their rooms by then. One of the young women had gone to stay in the room with

Armando. Francesca had thought about having him brought into her room, but he'd been asleep and she'd been afraid that moving him would only wake him.

When Marcos walked in, she could see the strain on his face. Her heart went out to him. How was it that this man, this wealthy man who controlled a vast empire, could be so broken up over one young girl whom he'd never even met?

She could explain it, because she knew Marcos, but there truly weren't enough words to do so. The way she'd fought for Jacques, the way she would have fought for her baby if she could have, this was the way he fought for these kids. With his whole heart, though she wasn't sure he realized that's what it was. He felt obligated, he'd said, because he'd been one of them.

But it was more than that. He could have turned out so cold and brutal after what had happened to him, but he wasn't.

He came over and caught her to him, sweeping her off her feet so quickly she gasped in surprise.

"No words, Francesca," he said. "I need you too much for words."

She didn't realize he'd carried her to his room until they were inside and he was whisking her shirt over her head. For some reason, the fact he'd taken her to *his* room caught at her heart and made hope blossom more strongly than before.

He stripped her urgently while she tore at his clothes in return. As soon as they were naked, they fell to the bed, mouths melding, limbs fusing, bodies straining for each other.

She was so turned on, so ready for him, that she didn't need any preliminaries. Wrapping her legs around his waist, she urged him inside her. When they were joined, she thought he would take her to the heights of pleasure very quickly, that his need was urgent.

Instead, he moved languidly, thoroughly, touching her so deeply that she could only gasp with each stroke. She'd never felt like this before, never felt her heart expanding so wide, the joy and pleasure of being with a man she loved so very much making the experience that much more intense.

What did Marcos feel when he was moving inside her like this? Did he feel the joy too? Or was it just the usual sort of pleasure a man felt in a woman's body?

He caught her face between his hands, forcing her to look at him as he made love to her. Her heart pounded in her chest, her temples, her throat. Surely he could see the way she felt shining in her eyes, hear it in the gasps and moans she couldn't help.

"You are beautiful, Francesca," he whispered. "Beautiful."

"Marcos, I—" She closed her eyes, swallowed. "I can't think…of anything…but you."

He kissed her—hot, wet, deep—stroking into her faster and faster until she finally shattered with a cry that felt like it had been ripped from her throat. The pleasure didn't stop there, however. Marcos slipped his hand between them and brought her to climax again, stroking her with his fingers and his body, this time following her over the edge when she went.

Soon, he rolled away, and though she mourned the loss of him, she welcomed the cool air rushing over her skin. He lay beside her, his chest rising and falling, his eyes closed. He was absolutely the sexiest thing she'd ever seen in her life. His body glistened with sweat, the hard muscles and smooth planes making her want to climb on top of him and repeat the experience.

To have all that to herself? To enjoy the power and beauty of a man like Marcos Navarre whenever she wanted? She was lucky, yes, but simply having sex with him wasn't enough. Would never be enough.

She'd never thought she would feel this way. After her baby died, part of her had died too. To feel love for someone, the kind of love that ripped you apart and sewed you back up again with every waking moment, was not something she'd been prepared for.

She studied his body without hesitation. He'd thrown an arm over his eyes. His hand lay against the pillow, his wrist turned out, the underside exposed. She leaned forward, studying the pale marks there. How had she not noticed this before? Marcos had very fine scars, so fine they weren't apparent until you were up close, in a band across his skin.

Carefully, she reached out and traced one finger along them. He flinched, but did not jerk away as he'd done in the past. Then she traced the scar on his abdomen. He dropped his arm, his eyes glittering as he watched her.

"You said you would make those men bleed for me, Marcos. And I would take the pain of these away, if I could."

"I know you would." He caught her fingers in his, kissed them. "I am sorry for what happened to you, Francesca. I can't help but think if I hadn't come into your life, it would have turned out differently."

"And if your uncle had never betrayed your parents and bartered the Corazón del Diablo to my father, perhaps my life would have been different. Or perhaps not."

"Have you always been so stoic?"

"Definitely not." She turned toward him, traced the line of his arm until she was at his wrist again. "Will you tell me what this is from?"

He closed his eyes, the pain on his features apparent. "I've never told anyone."

"Tell me."

"It's brutal, Francesca. Ugly."

"You mean ugly like being beaten so badly you lose your baby and can never have another one?"

He swore. She didn't think that was a good sign, but then he said, "I was captured by the enemy, chained in a dark room for days on end with no food, minimal water, and every incentive in the world to escape." He lifted his wrists, turned them out so she could see the fine markings on both. "I did not succeed, by the way."

Her heart was pounding for an entirely different reason now. She'd handcuffed him to a bed, for God's sake! She remembered the way he'd looked at her, the hatred in his eyes then. She'd humiliated him, forced him to recall his worst memories while she'd taken the Corazón del Diablo and disappeared into the night. No wonder he'd been so angry when he'd tracked her down.

"They beat me for information, but I did not give it to them. And they left me in the dark with rats and snakes coming in through the crumbling walls." He laughed, but there was no humor in it. "I spent one night with a python curled next to me for warmth. Why it didn't strangle me, I still don't know."

"Oh, Marcos," she breathed, tears pricking the backs of her eyes.

"I've seen too much ugliness, Francesca. And I suppose it's right you know, because you need to understand that I'm not capable of love, not really. I had it burned out of me in the hell of my life."

Pain wound around her heart, squeezed. "I don't believe that."

He pushed her back on the pillows, his handsome, tortured face hovering so close above hers. "Believe it, Francesca." His head dipped, his lips touching the hollow of her throat where her pulse beat hard and strong. "I am capable of this," he murmured, his tongue touching her pulse point, "of passion and sex. And I do want you. But I don't love you. I can't."

Though he was soon inside her again, taking her to the edge of pleasure and beyond with his skillful lovemaking, it didn't feel nearly as joyful as it had the last time.

Marcos bolted upright in bed, the dregs of the nightmare fading almost immediately as Francesca stirred beside him. She didn't wake, and he thought with some amazement that perhaps he hadn't cried out. Or maybe she was simply exhausted from their lovemaking. He'd taken much from her in his quest to drive the memory of tonight's events from his head.

Poor Ana Luis. Her body had been smashed almost beyond recognition in the single-car accident that claimed both her and the boy who was the son of a neighboring vintner. As horrible as those memories were, the image of Francesca rocking little Armando, who was now an orphan, and her quiet insistence on learning all of Marcos's deepest secrets with just a soft word and equally soft touch, were the primary things on his mind.

He'd told her everything. He had no secrets from this woman, and that alarmed him in some respects. How was it possible he'd told her those things?

But he had—and oddly enough, it made the burden somewhat lighter. Not much, but a little.

His heart still pounded from the dream, but not as fiercely as usual. For once, he couldn't even remember the specifics of the dream. He lay back down, curled around the warm woman next to him. Her back was to him, her beautiful naked buttocks thrust against his groin.

His cock stirred, but it was only out of proximity to her naked body and not because he wasn't satiated already. In fact, he didn't think he *could* make love again tonight. He wrapped his arms around her, happy in a way he'd not been in a long time to have a woman nestled against him. This woman.

He hadn't lied when he'd told her he was incapable of love, but he acknowledged that he did feel something for her. Something beyond what he usually felt for the women who shared his bed.

She was more of a kindred spirit, in some respects. He kissed her shoulder, drew in a breath scented with whatever flowery shampoo she used. Her hair was a gorgeous tumble of silk. He drew it aside, up and out of the way, and pressed his lips to the back of her neck. She stirred in her sleep, made a little mewling sound that made him hard when he'd thought it was probably impossible again tonight.

How had he missed the lush beauty of her figure

before? Even with forty extra pounds, she couldn't have hidden these curves away. But he'd been fooled by the baggy clothes and shyness, just as everyone else had been. Her sister must have known Francesca was the real beauty, that Francesca would someday outshine her, and she'd been evil because of it.

He'd always believed Francesca was as duplicitous in their first marriage as her family had been, but now he wasn't so sure. And, even if she was, she'd certainly paid enough for it, hadn't she?

It killed him to think she'd suffered so much. Because he'd taken the Corazón del Diablo and alienated her from her family. She'd have never been working in a jewelry store, never been in a position to be attacked so brutally, had her family kept their fortune and she remained a debutante.

But what choice had there been? The jewel was his, the symbol of his family and the touchstone of their memory. He'd have sold his soul to the devil to regain it.

Though, thinking about it, perhaps he already had.

Francesca turned in his arms then, her lips finding the sensitive spot beneath his ear, her tongue tracing the column of his neck and settling into the hollow of his throat. Marcos groaned as she rolled him onto his back and straddled his erect penis.

So much for being incapable again tonight.

Thank God.

The next day, when the house was still in mourning and arrangements to bury Ana were being made, Magdalena and her family came for a visit. Francesca instantly liked Marcos's sister. She was a sweet, sunny personality, and she expressed sympathy and horror over the news about Ana's death.

Francesca could tell she adored Marcos, who seemed to adore her equally. He'd said he wasn't capable of love, but clearly he was mistaken. He played with the children, held the baby, and gave everyone presents.

When Magdalena asked if Francesca wanted to hold her newborn, Marcos shot her a frown. In spite of her determination not to let her silly heart see hope where there was none, that gesture alone flooded her with warmth. He knew it might be hard on her and he was prepared to intervene with some excuse if she gave him reason.

"Of course I would," she said, taking little Amelia in her arms. The baby was red-faced and wide-eyed, and Francesca held her close, breathing in the scent of powder and newborn. It hurt to hold such a tiny baby— but maybe it hurt a little less than she'd thought it would only a few days before.

Cutting herself off from children until now had been necessary, but she felt as if she were ready to be around them again, as if the joy and love they brought weren't necessarily denied her forever.

As Marcos's involvement with his Foundation had brought home to her, there were still children who needed parents. She would never have her own child, but that didn't mean she had to be childless if she chose not to be.

Once Magdalena and her husband and children had gone again, Marcos returned to his office and left her to her own devices. She spent time with Armando and then went for a walk in the vineyard. Her emotions were so tangled and torn.

She loved Marcos, but he'd said he did not love her.

Could never love her. How could she manage the next three months this way?

How could she not?

There was no easy answer to that question. She wanted to spend every moment she could with him, wring every moment of happiness out of the situation, and hope for the best. And she wanted to escape at the same time, before she was crushed by the futility of loving a man who did not love her.

The rest of the week passed uneventfully enough, other than the sadness surrounding the funeral of a sixteen-year-old girl. Everyone from the winery turned out for the service. Ana was buried in a beautiful little cemetery near town. Marcos spared no expense, and the service was dignified and solemn. There would be no pauper's grave for the poor girl from the streets.

The funeral saddened Francesca and made her anxious. When she returned to the *bodega*, she called Gilles. He seemed surprised to hear from her, but the news he gave her was good. Jacques's doctors were pleased with his response to treatment thus far, though he was not out of the woods yet. He had a long road ahead, but everything seemed hopeful. Gilles had hired another jeweler, and a manager to run the business, and all was proceeding very well.

She hung up feeling both relieved and a bit wistful. The shop was doing great without her. After nearly eight years with Jacques, Gilles and a new crew could take the place over without her being missed at all. It was almost as if she'd had no imprint at all.

"What is wrong, *querida*?" Marcos asked.

Francesca had been so lost in thought that she hadn't realized he'd walked in. "I was just talking to Gilles.

He says Jacques is doing well, and the shop is running smoothly."

"And this is something to look worried about?"

"I was just thinking that they didn't need me. It was an odd feeling."

"You are needed here."

But he didn't mean it the way she wanted him to mean it. "Only for the next couple of months," she replied more crisply than she'd meant to.

Marcos either didn't notice or purposely ignored the dig. "We are retuning to Buenos Aires in the morning," he said. "I've been away from my business for too long as it is."

Her heart began to throb. "What about baby Armando? Will he come with us?"

Marcos shook his head, his hands shoved in the pockets of the crisp black trousers he'd worn to the funeral. "I am working on finding him a home, but for now I think it's best he stay here where he is familiar with everything."

Francesca gaped at him. "He's a toddler, Marcos. He's familiar with us. We could take care of him—"

"No," he cut in almost brutally. "Do not think we are taking this child, Francesca. He needs a permanent home, and he needs people who will not abandon him when he's come to love them."

She slapped a hand to her chest. "*I* wouldn't abandon him."

"Ah, but you will when our marriage contract is up."

CHAPTER TWELVE

BUENOS AIRES WAS a shock to the senses after the high desert beauty of Mendoza and the wine country. But even more of a shock was the reality of her situation with Marcos. They'd made love every night at the winery, they'd spent days walking in the vineyard, talking about Ana and the Foundation and the kids that it helped. They'd spent hours with Armando, playing with him, taking him for a sunny picnic once under the lone olive tree, and tucking him in at night.

In short, they'd played a happy family and she'd let herself be sucked in by the performance. No matter that he'd said he didn't love her, she'd thought surely he must love little Armando, that he would want her to stay and help him take care of the child.

Instead, he planned to let someone else adopt the boy.

Stupid, stupid, stupid. She'd been stupid to let herself believe, because when it came down to it, Marcos was not going to want to stay married to a woman who couldn't have his children.

And she didn't blame him, not really. He deserved children of his own, and she was not the woman who could ever give that to him. This was not a permanent marriage and would never be so. Marcos was under no delusions about the reality of it, while she kept trying to convince herself that he cared and that things could change given time.

As the day wore on, Francesca realized how much she missed little Armando. How could you fall in love with a child in a week? But she had, and while she didn't doubt that Marcos wanted the best for him too, she was sick to think that she'd never see the little boy again.

Marcos returned from his offices downtown sometime around eight that evening. Francesca had not heard from him since they'd touched down that morning and he'd gone to Navarre Industries' headquarters. She was watching television in the living area when he stalked in and tossed his briefcase and suit jacket on one of the couches.

Her heart always leapt at the sight of him, but now her joy was tinged with hurt and sadness. He picked up the remote and clicked the mute button.

"We are having a cocktail party here tomorrow evening," he said without preamble. "I need you to coordinate the menu with the chef. You will also need to choose a suitable dress since you will be wearing the Corazón del Diablo."

Francesca blinked. Anger began to build like a kettle on a low flame. "And what is this cocktail party for?"

"It's business—but there will be a couple attending who I've been told cannot conceive. They may be perfect for Armando."

"You certainly waste no time," she said crisply.

He looked puzzled. "You would be happier if this was not a top priority to find Armando a loving family?"

"I didn't say that. But you seem to think that choosing a family is rather like going to a store and picking out a new suit."

He shoved a hand through his hair. "I don't know what you expect from me, Francesca. I won't let just anyone adopt Armando. They are a possibility, not a definite choice."

What could she say? That she was angry and hurt because he wanted to find the child a loving home? What sense did that make?

None, of course. But it went deeper than that. It was about them as a couple, about the death knell of her dreams. It hurt to be faced with the reality of his feelings for her.

Marcos's expression changed. Grew softer, pitying even. "Francesca, I'm sorry if this hurts you. But I have to find a home for him. He is my responsibility. I know you grew close to him, but you will not always be in his life. Surely you can see how this is a problem?"

"Of course," she said, because there was nothing else to say.

Marcos nodded. "Good, I'm glad you agree."

But she did not. Instead, she hurt inside, hurt for all that would never be. For what she would never have.

And she realized, as the pain wrapped its tentacles around her heart, she couldn't do this. She couldn't stay here for the next couple of months, sharing Marcos's bed, hostessing his parties, living with him and loving him and knowing he did not feel the same. Would never feel the same.

Because she was damaged, and though she believed he was very sorry for what had happened to her, he would never be able to love her, to have her as his wife when she could not give him the children who would inherit his empire someday.

And she just couldn't live with that knowledge anymore. She had to leave, and she had to do it soon.

"I think I'll go to bed now," she said, standing.

Marcos's expression was carefully blank. "Goodnight, Francesca. We'll talk more in the morning."

She didn't trust herself to speak, so she inclined her head in reply. Then she turned her back and walked away.

Marcos didn't go to her bed that night, though he ached to do so. But she was angry with him, he knew, and it bothered him far too much that she was. He stayed away because he wanted to prove to himself he could do so, that Francesca had no real pull on him other than the desire that constantly pounded through his veins.

He wanted her, but he would be disciplined about it. Besides, a night alone would do them both good, would help to clear their heads about everything that had happened at the *Bodega Navarre*.

He'd loved spending time with her, and though their stay had been tinged by tragedy, there had been real joy in being there with her. She'd been a rock through the whole ordeal, and she'd helped to take care of the baby though it had surely made her think of the child she'd lost. He'd admired her very much then, and he'd even let himself consider what it would be like to tear up their contract and convince her to stay with him.

Because he enjoyed her company, craved her body,

and felt more at ease with her than he ever had with anyone. It was as if she understood him.

But on the day of the funeral, when they'd stood at the gravesite and watched the coffin being lowered into the ground, he'd realized he couldn't ask her to stay. She deserved better. She deserved a man who wasn't so damaged by life that he could never love her, and she deserved to have a home and, yes, even an adopted family if she chose.

He'd known, looking into her eyes that night, what she'd wanted from him. She'd wanted him to say they could keep Armando, could live as a family together, and though part of him strongly wanted to do so, he'd done what had to be done.

It was the right thing to do. Francesca would thank him someday.

The next morning, he breakfasted with her. She was aloof and distracted, he thought, but she was no doubt still hurt. She fidgeted with her food, pushing it around on the plate, before she finally speared him with golden-green eyes.

"I'm leaving, Marcos," she said.

He ignored the funny little flip his heart did. "Where are you going?"

"Back to New York."

He wanted to howl. "We have a contract, *querida*."

"I know. And I also know you won't cease Jacques's care. That was my only incentive to stay, when I thought you would do so. But you're too good, Marcos. As angry as you might be with me, you won't hurt someone you can help."

"I might," he said, though it was an empty threat. "The Corazón del Diablo—"

"Is yours. I will write you a letter stating my family has no claim and never has. I didn't want it, Marcos. I only wanted the money to take care of Jacques. Now that I don't need it, I don't care."

"Will you at least tell me why?"

She dropped her gaze to her lap and swallowed. Then she looked at him again, her heart shining in her eyes. "Because I love you. Because I want you to have what makes you happy, Marcos, and I've realized that it's not me. And I can't stay here with you when I know it's hopeless. If you care for me at all, even just a little bit, you have to let me leave."

He felt as if someone was squeezing a giant vise around his chest. He didn't want to let her go, not yet. But how could he not? He'd upended her life once before when she'd thought she loved him. He could not in good conscience do so again. It was wrong, so very wrong to keep her here simply to suit his own needs.

No matter how much he wanted to.

"Very well," he said, the words scraping his throat like sandpaper. "I will make the arrangements."

Snow had come early to New York that year. The sidewalks were blanketed in a crisp layer of white, and everything looked magical and fresh.

Francesca was numb, but not from cold. She'd been back for three weeks and she hadn't heard from Marcos at all. She'd made it through that last day with him, hosted the cocktail party gowned in a gorgeous ruby red dress and wearing the Corazón del Diablo, and met the very sweet couple who would probably become Armando's parents.

Marcos had smiled and mingled as if nothing was wrong, and her heart had cracked every time she'd heard him laugh. He'd agreed so easily to her request. So easily that she knew she truly meant nothing to him. A part of her had harbored the hope that he would refuse, that he would be forced to realize she meant something to him after all.

He had not. The next morning, she hadn't even seen him before the car arrived and it was time to go. It was as if he'd cut her from his life completely once he'd agreed to her request.

Francesca walked down the street with her collar turned up and her eyes fixed on the sidewalk in front of her. Soon, the snow would turn black with dirt and foot-prints—which would certainly match her mood more accurately.

A pang of longing for the warmth of the high desert in Mendoza sliced through her. Worse, a pang of long-ing for the man who'd shared those glorious days with her rode hard on its heels. She thought about Armando, wondered if he was in his new home yet. She hoped he would be happy and healthy and have the kind of life his mother would have wanted for him.

Marcos had not called or sent any form of commu-nication since she'd left Argentina. She had expected divorce papers, but it was still early. They could be de-livered any day now.

At least there was a bright spot in her otherwise dreary life. Jacques's condition was improving tremendously. He was actually beginning to get color back into his cheeks. He was coming home in a few days, though he would have to return twice weekly for treatment.

A nurse would be accompanying him for around-the clock-care.

One more thing for which to be grateful to Marcos. Jacques wasn't out of the woods yet, but the doctors grew more optimistic each day.

Francesca took the steps up to her apartment and let herself in, unwinding her scarf and dropping it onto a chair. She shrugged out of her coat and hung it up, then went to the kitchen to check on the soup she'd left simmering at the back of the stove.

How easily she'd slipped back into her normal life— and how strange and empty it all seemed.

The buzzer to the downstairs door rang. She went to the intercom and, once she'd determined it was a deliveryman, let him inside. Dread pooled in the pit of her stomach as she stood on the landing. Could it be the divorce papers?

The man came up the steps with a small package clutched beneath one arm. He had her sign an electronic form, keyed in some information, and handed the parcel to her. Francesca thanked him, then went inside and took the package to the counter in the kitchen.

There was no return address, and she had no idea who might send her something express delivery.

Though perhaps it was something from the hospital. Something of Jacques's. She grabbed a pair of scissors from a drawer and sliced into the cardboard.

A velvet box lay nestled among the air packets. She lifted it out, puzzled. When she flipped open the lid, her heart skidded to a stop before it began to beat double time.

The fiery yellow glow of the gemstone winking at

her from a sea of white diamonds was unmistakable.
She snatched up the folded note that lay beneath the
Corazón del Diablo.

   Come to the Four Seasons. There is a car waiting.
Marcos

CHAPTER THIRTEEN

MARCOS STOOD ON the fifty-first floor, gazing out of the window of this luxurious suite, and wondered if she would come.

Of course she will come.

He'd sent the necklace as a gesture of his surrender. But was it too subtle? Would she be so angry with him that she would not take the chance?

He scraped a hand through his hair and blew out a breath. He eyed the handcuffs he'd bought.

Could he really do what he planned to do?

Yes, because she will come.

Francesca had said she loved him, and he'd held onto those words for the past three weeks. They'd rung through his head every minute of every day. At first, he'd believed that letting her go was the right thing to do.

But nothing had been the same once she'd gone. He'd watched from a window as she'd climbed into the car, feeling numb. Then he'd made himself watch as the car pulled into the street and disappeared into traffic.

He'd stood there for a long time after, envisioning the journey to the airport, wondering what Francesca was thinking.

Was she hating him now? Congratulating herself on a lucky escape?

Or was she crying?

She was brave and tough, his little tiger kitten. The thought of her crying twisted his heart into a knot. He didn't want to make her cry.

He'd tried to push her from his mind as the days dragged by, tried to continue running his business and the Foundation.

But she'd left a hollow spot inside him with her absence. He'd thought it would fill up slowly, but it never did. The hole grew bigger with each passing day, until he realized what a fool he'd been.

He had to win her back. Determined, he turned and picked up the cuffs. She would come, and he would prove to her that he needed her, that he could be the man she deserved.

Francesca hadn't bothered to change out of her jeans and sweater before shoving the jewel box in her purse and bounding outside to the idling limo that waited at the curb. Now that she'd arrived, however, she was beginning to regret that she'd not taken time to make herself look a bit more presentable.

The grand foyer, with its rows of tall columns and gleaming surfaces, was understatedly elegant. And she was completely out of place. She'd hoped Marcos would meet her in the lobby, but instead she was pointed to the elevators and given an access key with a room number printed on it.

She rode the elevator up to the fifty-first floor. Thank goodness he'd not stayed here the first time, or she'd never have been able to get inside. When she entered the luxurious Presidential suite, it was quiet except for the hiss and crackle of the gas fireplace in the living room. Was he even here?

"Marcos?" she called.

"In here."

She followed his voice, emerging into a bedroom with spectacular views of Central Park and the night sky. But that wasn't what caught her attention.

Marcos was on the bed, fully clothed, leaning against the headboard. One arm was raised over his head. His wrist was cuffed to the bedpost.

"What are you doing?" she cried.

He smiled, though the scar at the corner of his mouth was white. "Therapy."

She hurried over to his side, dropping her purse on the floor. "Where is the key?"

"I'm not quite sure. I threw it out of reach before I closed the cuff. I did not wish to chicken out, as you Americans say."

"Marcos, that's insane!" She turned in a circle, looking for a slice of silver in the dim lamplight.

"Perhaps, but I had to do something."

She popped her hands on her hips and glared at him. "There are many things you could do about it, but this probably wasn't the best idea. What if I hadn't come?"

"I knew you would."

"What if I hadn't been home? What if I hadn't got the package tonight? They'd have taken it back to the warehouse and attempted redelivery tomorrow."

"I had faith."

Francesca rolled her eyes. "My God, Marcos, couldn't you have simply picked up the phone?"

He looked suddenly wary. "I was afraid you wouldn't listen."

"And this is designed to make me listen?" She turned away, intent on finding the key. Marcos didn't say anything, and she knew he was fighting with himself. Trying not to panic, she was certain.

Her heart pounded so hard. The blood rushed in her ears, drowning out sound. She had to find that key, had to free him. Knowing what she did, she couldn't stand to see him like this. He may think trial by fire was therapy—a typical alpha male way of approaching things—but it was killing her to know he was in pain.

Falling to her hands and knees, she patted the carpet. When she felt something small and cool, she snatched it up. Her hands shook as she inserted the key into the lock. Marcos leaned toward her, his face practically touching her breasts as she worked the catch. Desire flared to life inside her as he took a deep breath.

"You smell good, *mi gatita.*"

The lock clicked and the cuff snapped open. Marcos put both arms around her before she could take a step away.

"I have missed you," he said.

She put her hands on his shoulders, pushing until his grip loosened. Then she pulled away and wrapped her arms around her middle.

"You are angry with me," he said.

"A bit." And hurt. And confused. And unsure she wanted to relive even a moment of pleasure with him if it was only going to lead to more heartbreak.

Because he did want her, she knew that. But it was a physical need, not an emotional one. Had he really called her here just to get in her panties again? After this stunt, she truly had no idea what he was capable of.

"You have every right to be," he said. "I understand this."

"Then why are you here? Do you feel guilty? Want to ease your troubled conscience?" She was surprised to find that anger was indeed the dominant emotion she felt at the moment. Because she really didn't know what he wanted. He'd dragged her here with the Corazón del Diablo and a note, but he'd not fallen to his knees and proclaimed his undying love, or said he needed her in his life, or anything else.

Instead, he'd chained himself to the bed and scared her half to death in the process.

"The nightmares are back," he said softly. He stood and shoved his hands in his pockets. "They are even worse now, in some ways."

"And you thought that chaining yourself to this bed and hoping I would come along might help?"

"Perhaps not the best plan, but I'm working on it."

She shook her head. "How is it possible the dreams are worse?"

"Because you are in them, and it is you I cannot save."

"I'm fine, I assure you."

"I can see that. But without you, I do not sleep well."

"And what is the solution to that? That I return to Argentina and sleep with you every night?"

"*Sí.*"

Francesca blinked. "For how long?"

He shrugged. "As long as it takes."

"No." Damn him! How dare he come along and entice

her with such a thing, and all because he slept better when she was there? "Ask some other woman."

He shoved a hand through his hair. "Clearly, I am doing this wrong."

"Clearly."

He caught her by the shoulders, gripping her too hard for her to get away easily but not so hard it hurt. "I need you, Francesca. I was a fool to let you go."

Her eyes filled with tears. It was what she wanted to hear—but after so much pain and heartbreak, how could she believe it? She'd believed in him before, and she'd been wrong.

"What changed your mind? Nightmares? Because I'm not sure that's enough, Marcos."

He let her go, walked over to the windows and gazed out at the nightlights of the city. His shoulders seemed to sag a little.

"I'm afraid, Francesca. Afraid because for the first time in my life, I actually care about someone else's happiness and well being more than my own." He turned to face her again. "I know I've not done this well, and I know you have reason not to trust me, but I'm trying to tell you that I love you. As deeply and as much as I am able."

A tear slid down her cheek and she dashed it away. "Why should that be so hard to say?" she asked, her throat aching.

"Because I know I'm not a good bargain. Part of me is ruined and broken. It's unfair to ask you to fix that, but you are the only one who can. Without you, I'm lost. And I know this is selfish of me, but I want you to come back."

Her legs refused to hold her upright any longer. She

sank onto the end of the bed and stared at him. "I love you, Marcos, but I'm scared too. Because I can never have children, and you are a man who deserves to have his own children. How do I know you won't resent me for it later? That you won't regret this once you feel like the damage of the past is repaired? Because it's not me who will repair it, but you. I really have nothing to do with it."

"You have *everything* to do with it. If you hadn't come into my life again, I wouldn't have understood that I have the strength to move beyond my past. You taught me that." He came over to her then, knelt before her and took her hands in his. His handsome face was so serious. "And you of all people should know that a family is built on love, not genetics. Is Jacques any less your family because you are not related? Do your mother and sister have a greater claim on your affections because they share your blood?"

She shook her head. The lump in her throat was too big to speak. She thought of her mother, her cold cruel mother in her drafty house with her mantle of blame, and knew what he said was right. Just because someone gave birth to you did not mean they were capable of loving you.

He squeezed her hands. "Do you know why I sent you the Corazón del Diablo?"

"No," she managed.

"Because possessing it has caused me nothing but sorrow. It *is* the devil's heart, and it exacts a great price. And I'm tired of being a prisoner to my past. I want to go forward, and I want to do this with you."

"How is giving me the necklace letting go of the past?"

"Because you are free to do with it what you wish. Donate it to a museum, give it to Jacques—I don't care. But when you've done what you want, all I ask is that you come home with me. I need you."

Hope was unfurling in her soul, the wind of his words catching it and fanning it higher. Could she really dare to believe? "It's your birthright, Marcos. You can't just give it up like that. It means too much. You've fought too hard for it."

"I have already let it go," he said, his eyes so serious as they searched hers. "It's yours. As am I. The symbolism is meaningless without you."

But she had to be sure. "You would give up the possibility of ever having a biological child? It's not something to be done lightly, Marcos. I didn't have a choice, but you do."

He kissed her hands, then cupped the back of her head and kissed her lips. "I love you, Francesca. You make my world brighter. Whether or not you are able to give me a child of my blood has nothing to do with how I feel about you."

She shook her head, so scared and so uncertain—and so hopeful. "You'll regret it. You'll resent me later—"

"No, I won't. I cannot resent you when you are my heart, my soul. You make me whole again. I need you. Armando needs you."

"Armando?"

"He's had quite an upheaval, but he needs a stable life. We can give that to him. I want us to be the ones who give it to him."

"But I thought you had found him a family."

"He already has a family. Us, Ingrid and Isabelle. The *bodega* and everyone there."

She squeezed her eyes shut. "It's not fair to try and bribe me this way."

"I don't care about fair, *mi amor*. I care about you. I want to spend every day with you, talking, arguing, making love, going for walks, taking care of Armando. I want to wake up each day knowing you will be there. And I want you to know that I love you, and that I've never said those words to anyone other than my mother. Not anyone, Francesca. Not ever."

Her heart was expanding with all she felt. With every word he said, she believed him. She touched his face, traced the scar at his mouth. He turned his head, and kissed her palm.

"Please, Francesca," he said urgently. "I can't do this without you. Say you will come home with me, that you will love me—"

"I already do love you. So much it scares me."

"Then say you will marry me and be my wife forever."

"Luckily, we're already married," she said with a watery smile.

He answered her with a sexy grin. "Then we can start immediately on the honeymoon. My favorite part."

"Mine too."

"*Bueno,*" he said, tugging her sweater up. "Because I have much I wish to do to you before this night is through…"

It was a very wonderful night, Francesca thought. But not until much, much later…

EPILOGUE

HE TRULY WAS THE luckiest man in the world. Marcos sat on the veranda of the *Bodega Navarre*, gazing out at the vineyards and the laughing little boy playing with Francesca. Little Armando was a dynamo at three years old. He was quick, smart, and as adorable as ever.

Marcos loved him with all his heart. Though it saddened him to think of how the boy had come into their lives, he was very happy they were the ones who'd adopted the child once his mother had died so tragically. Armando would have a good life as a Navarre. And, when he was old enough, he would know about his mother. Both Marcos and Francesca agreed that was important.

Ingrid came to take Armando for his bath, and Francesca collapsed into a chair.

"Wore you out, did he?"

"Lord yes," she said, taking a sip of the cool lemon ice water one of the girls had brought out. He watched her, felt a well of emotion as she set the glass down and gave him a funny little look. "What?"

"I love you, Francesca. You are the most beautiful woman in the world."

"You don't have to keep telling me I'm beautiful.

We've been married for almost two years now. I'm not worried you'll let another woman turn your head."

"But you are beautiful. Extraordinarily so. I tell you this because I mean it." He leaned over and kissed her. "If you would like to retire for a *siesta*, I could show you how beautiful you are to me. I am aching to do so."

Her smile turned wicked. "Marcos Navarre, are you trying to corrupt me?"

"Every chance I get," he vowed. He pulled her onto his lap and kissed her. She made a little sound of pleasure in her throat when she discovered he was already hard for her.

"Oh my," she said. "I'm looking forward to that *siesta*."

"Let's go then."

"Do you two ever stop?"

Francesca jumped up and went to hug the old man who'd hobbled onto the veranda. "Jacques, how are you feeling? Did you sleep well?"

"I'm fine, sweetheart," he said.

She helped him into a chair and poured a glass of wine for him. "And your sleep?"

He took an appreciative sip. "I slept like an old man of seventy-seven should sleep. Stop fussing, Francesca. Now you two go on and do whatever you were going to do, don't mind me. I'll just sit here and enjoy the view."

"Then we will enjoy it with you," Marcos said without hesitation. Francesca smiled at him, and he thought once more what a lucky man he was. Tonight, he would show her just how he felt. And every night for the rest of their lives.

Coming Next Month

from **Harlequin Presents® EXTRA.** Available April 12, 2011.

Coming Next Month

from **Harlequin Presents®.** Available April 26, 2011.

Visit www.HarlequinInsideRomance.com
for more information on upcoming titles!

HPCNM0411

REQUEST YOUR FREE BOOKS!

2 FREE NOVELS PLUS 2 FREE GIFTS!

YES! Please send me 2 FREE Harlequin Presents® novels and my 2 FREE gifts (gifts are worth about $10). After receiving them, if I don't wish to receive any more books, I can return the shipping statement marked "cancel." If I don't cancel, I will receive 6 brand-new novels every month and be billed just $4.05 per book in the U.S. or $4.74 per book in Canada. That's a saving of at least 15% off the cover price! It's quite a bargain! Shipping and handling is just 50¢ per book in the U.S. and 75¢ per book in Canada.* I understand that accepting the 2 free books and gifts places me under no obligation to buy anything. I can always return a shipment and cancel at any time. Even if I never buy another book, the two free books and gifts are mine to keep forever.

106/306 HDN FC55

Name _____ (PLEASE PRINT)

Address _____ Apt. #

City _____ State/Prov. _____ Zip/Postal Code

Signature (if under 18, a parent or guardian must sign)

Mail to the **Reader Service:**
IN U.S.A.: P.O. Box 1867, Buffalo, NY 14240-1867
IN CANADA: P.O. Box 609, Fort Erie, Ontario L2A 5X3

Not valid for current subscribers to Harlequin Presents books.

**Are you a current subscriber to Harlequin Presents books
and want to receive the larger-print edition?
Call 1-800-873-8635 or visit www.ReaderService.com.**

* Terms and prices subject to change without notice. Prices do not include applicable taxes. Sales tax applicable in N.Y. Canadian residents will be charged applicable taxes. Offer not valid in Quebec. This offer is limited to one order per household. All orders subject to credit approval. Credit or debit balances in a customer's account(s) may be offset by any other outstanding balance owed by or to the customer. Please allow 4 to 6 weeks for delivery. Offer available while quantities last.

Your Privacy—The Reader Service is committed to protecting your privacy. Our Privacy Policy is available online at www.ReaderService.com or upon request from the Reader Service.

We make a portion of our mailing list available to reputable third parties that offer products we believe may interest you. If you prefer that we not exchange your name with third parties, or if you wish to clarify or modify your communication preferences, please visit us at www.ReaderService.com/consumerschoice or write to us at Reader Service Preference Service, P.O. Box 9062, Buffalo, NY 14269. Include your complete name and address.

HP11

*With an evil force hell-bent on destruction,
two enemies must unite to find a truth that turns
all-too-personal when passions collide.*

*Enjoy a sneak peek in Jenna Kernan's next installment
in her original* TRACKER *series, GHOST STALKER,
available in May, only from Harlequin Nocturne.*

"**W**ho are you?" he snarled.

Jessie lifted her chin. "Your better."

His smile was cold. "Such arrogance could only come from a Niyanoka."

She nodded. "Why are you here?"

"I don't know." He glanced about her room. "I asked the birds to take me to a healer."

"And they have done so. Is that *all* you asked?"

"No. To lead them away from my friends." His eyes fluttered and she saw them roll over white.

Jessie straightened, preparing to flee, but he roused himself and mastered the momentary weakness. His eyes snapped open, locking on her.

Her heart hammered as she inched back.

"Lead who away?" she whispered, suddenly afraid of the answer.

"The ghosts. Nagi sent them to attack me so I would bring them to her."

The wolf must be deranged because Nagi did not send ghosts to attack living creatures. He captured the evil ones after their death if they refused to walk the Way of Souls, forcing them to face judgment.

"Her? The healer you seek is also female?"

"Michaela. She's Niyanoka, like you. The last Seer of Souls and Nagi wants her dead."

Jessie fell back to her seat on the carpet as the possibility of this ricocheted in her brain. Could it be true?

"Why should I believe you?" But she knew why. His black aura, the part that said he had been touched by death. Only a ghost could do that. But it made no sense.

Why would Nagi hunt one of her people and why would a Skinwalker want to protect her? She had been trained from birth to hate the Skinwalkers, to consider them a threat.

His intent blue eyes pinned her. Jessie felt her mouth go dry as she considered the impossible. Could the trickster be speaking the truth? Great Mystery, what evil was this?

She stared in astonishment. There was only one way to find her answers. But she had never even met a Skinwalker before and so did not even know if they dreamed.

But if he dreamed, she would have her chance to learn the truth.

Look for GHOST STALKER by Jenna Kernan,
available May only from Harlequin Nocturne,
wherever books and ebooks are sold.

Harlequin *Romance*

*Don't miss an irresistible new trilogy
from acclaimed author*

SUSAN MEIER

IN THE BOARDROOM

Greek Tycoons become devoted dads!

Coming in April 2011
The Baby Project

Whitney Ross is terrified when she becomes guardian
to a tiny baby boy, but everything changes when
she meets dashing Darius Andreas, Greek tycoon
and now a brand-new daddy!

Second Chance Baby (May 2011)
Baby on the Ranch (June 2011)

Fan favorite author
TINA LEONARD
is back with
an exciting new miniseries.

Six bachelor brothers are given a challenge—
get married, start a big family and whoever does
so first will inherit the famed Rancho Diablo.
Too bad none of these cowboys is marriage material!

Callahan Cowboys:
Catch one if you can!

The Cowboy's Triplets (May 2011)
The Cowboy's Bonus Baby (July 2011)
The Bull Rider's Twins (Sept 2011)
Bonus Callahan Christmas Novella! (Nov 2011)
His Valentine Triplets (Jan 2012)
Cowboy Sam's Quadruplets (March 2012)
A Callahan Wedding (May 2012)

www.eHarlequin.com

HAR75358